Children of the Elementi

Ceri Clark

ISBN-13: 978-1-909236-02-8

ISBN-10: 1-909236-02-0

Lycan Books in association with Myrddin Publishing Group

Credits:

Editor: Alison DeLuca

Cover: Ceri Clark with eye and city component photos from BigStockPhoto.com

unique electronic & print books

Contact us at:

www.LycanBooks.com & www.MyrddinPublishingGroup.com

DEDICATION

I would like to thank my husband who has supported me through the years and everyone at Myrddin Publishing who have helped make this book happen.

CONTENTS

ACKNOWLEDGMENTS

I would like to give special thanks to my friend,
editor and talented author, Alison DeLuca.

Prologue:
End of an Empire

They crept down the dark corridor. The two darkly clad figures moved stealthily, throwing anxious glances behind them as they went. Dappled patterns of light and shadows played over the ancient stone walls from the torch the man carried, revealing a seemingly endless portrait gallery of long-dead royalty. Each painting hung in oppressive grandeur, the solemn faces seemed to reprove the pair as they passed.

Nuin kept her breaths shallow mindful that the sweet smell of the burning trika-wood torch only barely hid the underlying reek of the disused corridor. She wished they could have used glow-sticks, but they would have been missed. She sighed. If they wanted to warn her husband, this was the only way.

Nuin gasped as pain ripped through her. Her

hand grasped the wall and her knees buckled in a half-crouch.. Kiron, only a few steps ahead turned and lurched back to steady her.

"Are you well, my lady?"

He took in the drained paleness of her skin against her chestnut hair and blue velvet gown in the flickering light.

Nuin stroked the slight curve of her stomach, the only clue to her condition.

"I'm fine." She brushed tendrils of hair away from her eyes.

"We could have come through the front door, my lady." His voice held gentle reproach.

She shook her head. "We have to do this. You heard the Seer. There is danger somewhere. I- I'm not imagining it. We have to warn him."

Kiron touched her stomach and smiled with reassurance. Using his honed senses he began to check the baby's life signs. His awareness quickly shot through the upper layers of skin, through the rushing sound of his old friend's blood vessels and still further until he reached the smooth regular beat of the child's heart. He smiled again.

"He's fine. Although it's amazing that you still don't show, even after nearly six months."

"I wanted to surprise him. If my stomach was out here," Nuin extended her arms out in front of her. "I wouldn't have been able to. I hope we're not too late!"

Her eyes roved over the wall and her thoughts returned to the portraits. The color on each picture frame represented the five great families. On the right, she recognized the white frames of her husband's ruling family, and on the left, the colored frames of their consorts - many shared her own blue water element.

Kiron held out his arm and Nuin gratefully used it as a support to help her stand. She steadied herself for a moment more, fighting a brief spell of dizziness before they moved on again. It wasn't far to the inhabited part of the palace and within minutes they paused at an intersection. Nuin gratefully leant against the stone wall, savoring the coolness while Kiron edged forward to check the way ahead.

As he moved to round the corner, the door to the king's apartment creaked. Curious, Nuin quietly stepped nearer to the corner to stand beside Kiron. Who would visit this late? Her eyes widened in disbelief as her breath caught in her throat. She saw a figure leaving the royal apartment - the visitor - the long dark hair, the blue crystal around her neck - it was like looking in a mirror!

The woman halted mid-step and turned

sharply. Instinctively Nuin and Kiron scrambled back from view and held their breath as the woman's eyes narrowed. She seemed to examine the hallway. Kiron shook his head in disgust at himself and moved to challenge the stranger but Nuin's hand shot out and grabbed his arm. Shaking her head at him, her sharp gaze warned him to stay. He balked but nodded reluctantly in response. Searching for a moment more, the woman turned again and carried on down the corridor.

As the footsteps faded, Nuin straightened, shaken by the strange encounter. Who was that? What was that? She rushed to the open door. At the threshold, she paused. Where was Malo? Taking deep breaths to quell her rising panic, she scanned the room, looking for the familiar and reassuring shape of her husband.

At that moment she heard it. There was a groan from the far side of the room. She saw a hand slide away from the rich fabric covering the bed. She felt her lungs tighten in fear. What was happening? Rushing round the bed she saw her husband half-collapsed on the marble floor. He was clutching his chest, gasping for breath. Beside him lay a spilled wine cup.

"Poison," she breathed, "Kiron, come quickly."

Only seconds behind, Kiron brushed past her

to his liege's aid. Using his heightened senses he scanned the king's body. In his mind's eye, he could see the poison. It glowed with an evil, hot, vivid purple as the liquid ran unchecked through the king's blood. The deathly color spread slowly but steadily, he saw, and half of the king's body was already affected. Anguished, he knew there was nothing he could do. The poison had advanced too far. They were too late. He glanced at Nuin.

"I'm so sorry. I can only stop the pain. He has only a few minutes at most."

"Do it!" Tears flowed from her eyes.

Steeling himself, Kiron knelt beside Malo. The healer carefully lifted a flap on a small leather pouch that hung around his waist. His fingers shook with nerves but he held them with his other hand to still them as he glanced at Nuin to see if she had noticed. He took a deep breath and picked out a small green crystal, he cupped the jewel in his hands and held it up to his eyes, simultaneously relaxing his muscles as he began to concentrate into its depths. A swirl of dark green answered his call and he felt his powers gather focus and grow.

As they grew, he directed the energy into the king and began to synchronize with the other man. Kiron could feel the pain the king suffered while he blocked the other man's emotions. The agony nearly blinded him, and he fought for control. The pain built in intensity, and he had to fight to concentrate. Slowly, linked to Malo's mind, he began to create a virtual wall. Brick by brick it grew to trap the pain behind. As he imagined placing the last brick, both men visibly relaxed.

Already weak from using his ability, Kiron again gasped. He stumbled backwards from renewed pain but caught himself on the edge of the bed.

"Sephone! I can't feel her anymore!" he explained as Nuin tore her eyes from her husband. A profound sense of loss almost overwhelmed him. "The Earth Queen is dead, something is really wrong. We have to go."

Nuin shrugged Kiron's hand off her shoulder.

"I cannot leave Malo."

"You must go for the sake of our son." Malo took hold of an elaborate gold chain from round his neck. "Make certain he gets this. He will not be able to rule without it."

Nuin frowned, reaching out for the chain as she reached for the necklace. "You knew?"

He smiled back, "Of course I knew. I have the powers of all the elements. Listen, you need to go to the Citadel. I was expecting something to happen but I honestly thought we had enough guards here or I would never have called all the Elementi into one place. I never thought... I never considered this kind of trickery. I can already feel the absence of Earth and Fire in the Matrix. Both Sephone and Vilcin must be dead. The Magi have finally found their way in."

As Malo spoke, Nuin felt a sharp wrench in her chest as though the core of her being was ripping apart - Father! All thoughts ceased as the pain became unbearable but as quickly as it started, it ended leaving her trembling. As her eyes cleared, she tried to deny the death of her father. The Water King! How could this have happened now? He was so strong, he should have been a match for any traitor, but with Malo weakened, she choked at the thought. If he was dying, then they wouldn't be able to join their powers. She looked down at her husband. Everything should have been perfect, the Empire was at peace, their baby would have been the future. She never even had a chance to tell her father about him. Nuin couldn't comprehend how this could have happened. The Elementi had become too trusting and now three of the most high were dead. She looked again at her husband for answers but his body lay lifeless.

Before she could take it in, Kiron grasped her arm and pulled Nuin away from the fallen High-King,

"We have to go! Your child is our only hope; he is the last of the Omnax line. We have to go before they close the Gate. We must get to the Citadel!"

Dazed, she let Kiron guide her away from her husband's body. They could both hear the distant clash of swords through the ancient oak door. She stared widely about the room. There were no secret passages, the walls were solid stone. The rich hangings taunted her of safe locations through the Empire. Each wall depicted a vista from the four lands, the plains of the Earth Queen, the Mer City on another wall. Although beautiful, she also knew they were there to help visualize a place to escape to but she didn't have the technology to transport there. The sounds of pursuit were coming closer. There was something about the tapestries she had to remember... Nuin pulled a ring off her hand. She stared at it in wonder as an idea began to take root.

"No need. Before Malo left for the city last month, he gave me this ring. I couldn't understand why at the time." She stroked the clear jewel. "Only an Omnax power should be able to use this and I only have the water talent. Although if Malo knew about the baby, perhaps... I might be able to tap the baby's powers? Why would he give it to me otherwise...?"

Unsure but knowing she had to at least try, Nuin looked inward. She felt the strong pulse and the tiny thread of magic running inside her small baby's veins. As she was taught as a child, she pictured the four different elements as colors. There was red for fire, green for earth, yellow for air. Last, her own blue element of water answered her call, as familiar as an old friend. As the colors entwined together to make a strong white cord of power, she clutched the ring and called the energy to it.

There were sudden, loud footsteps in the hall outside. She knew they had no time to spare. She looked at Kiron but he was already running to the half-open door. He kicked it closed and heaved a heavy cabinet in front. Once the room was secured, he took Nuin's hand.

With one last tearful glimpse at her husband, she grabbed Kiron's arm tightly and made one final push with her mind. She felt the cord resist. Panic flashed in her mind as the door visible above the cabinet in front of them splintered. She grew cold with fear as the tip of a sword broke through, announcing the invader's arrival at the door. She pushed again, praying to any god who would listen.

The world exploded into fragments and a bright blinding light overtook them.

CHAPTER ONE
- JAKE

Jake blocked out the sound of shouts from downstairs and carried on tapping on his keyboard. Every night! His parents had never been like that.

He slammed his hands on his keyboard and stared glumly at the nonsense he had just written. The essay would never get done. In frustration, he deleted everything he had just written.

He heard another loud smash from downstairs and winced. Another plate gone. It was a good thing he had hidden her good china last week! The way Aunt Emma threw dishes, there would be nothing left. Although she really had to improve her aim. Uncle Ben was far too good at dodging. He grinned.

This had been coming for months. His uncle

was so clumsy; it had only been a matter of time before Aunt Emma found out. Giving up on the assignment, Jake opened his browser. As he was typing his password into his favorite site, Chatlite pinged. Karl was finally online.

Karl359: Waz up?

Tech_Warrior: Not much. The Richards are at it again.

Karl359: at least they don't shout at you!!

Tech_Warrior: only cos I don't exist to them. lol

Karl359: The video?

Tech_Warrior: No, They might hear I'm not doing homework :-)

Karl359: K, have you had a chance to look at Battle Land yet? There are some great moves we could copy for next week.

Tech_Warrior: No, I'm bored though, I might as well have a look.

Karl359: K, I've sent you the link by email. You'll lose it otherwise!

Karl359: Did you get the answers for the science test tomorrow?

Tech_Warrior: You know it doesn't work like that. He was thinking about the periodic tables and something 2 do with compounds, before D distracted him.

Karl359: cool. At least it narrows it down. Here's that link. I'll let N know tonight. He should leave us alone for a few days.

"Jake!" Aunt Emma's shriek reverberated from downstairs.

Tech_Warrior: M's calling. b4n. C u later.
Karl359: K

Rushing downstairs, Jake found Emma alone in the lounge. She sat in her favorite chair, staring into the gentle flames of the gas fire. Her eyes were red; she'd been crying again. As Jake reached to push the door open, he recoiled in surprise. The turmoil from her mind hit him like an icy blast. Without any conscious effort on his part, his aunt's thoughts became clearer.

He'd tried to explain it to Karl. How he could almost hear people talking to him even though he knew they weren't. It came and went, too quickly to harness. Jake moved forward to read her surface thoughts before it disappeared again. It seemed this time she thought Ben was gone for good. Jake shook his head in disgust. He knew it was just another argument. It happened almost every other day. She always thought Ben was going to leave. "Chance would be a fine thing," he grumbled under his breath.

Normally he could only hear thoughts for a few seconds, but for some reason he could still hear her. Aunt Emma was obviously more upset than usual. Whatever, he did not want to hear it. Jake turned to leave the room. He didn't want to invade her privacy any more than he had to. He *liked* Aunt Emma. But he 'heard' her think about him and... what was it? Adoption...? ...in the same thought - ...what?

"Aunt Emma?"

"Oh Jake, you took your time." She smiled weakly and turned to face him. "I need you to pop out and get me some stamps. Are you out tonight?"

"No, I'll just stay in my room again," he bluffed.

Emma paused.

"Well next time you 'stay in your room', do make sure you close your window properly as you leave. Ben nearly caught you yesterday. I had to go to your room to stop the shutter banging. I know you need your freedom, so I covered for you." Emma dissolved in tears. "That's if he comes back."

"He will, don't worry." Jake pulled up a stool and shoved a pile of Ben's car magazines on the floor. The box of tissues was underneath them.

He had to find out about the adoption. Were Ben and Emma going to adopt someone?

"Is anyone in our family adopted?"

Emma stared at Jake, tissue halfway to her eyes. Jake concentrated on her thoughts. They were flitting about. He saw Ben in her mind telling her never to tell him. They were in their old house in London. Jake had never seen it but he had seen pictures. Never tell him what? She was trying to work out how he knew. He prodded her thoughts, *What?* ... and her mind darted to a will hidden in the room. Unconsciously, her eyes strayed to the bay window and he saw where it was hidden in her mind.

Emma stood quickly and swept past Jake. She paused in the doorway, "Don't be silly. I don't know what you're talking about. There's some money on the table for the stamps. Don't be too long. Your tea will be ready in one hour."

Stunned, Jake sat there for a moment. He was adopted? How? Why hadn't his parents said anything? He tried to deny what he had just discovered, but it was clear in her mind. How could his parents not have *told* him? Shaking his head to clear it, he picked up the five-pound note from the coffee table, grabbed his coat and headed for the back door. What was going on? He had 'seen' where his aunt and uncle kept his parents' will. Tonight, he decided. He would look for it while his aunt and uncle were asleep. Adoption was far more important than just another beach party.

Later in his room, Jake waited until he heard the click of the landing light. *Great, they were in bed.* Quietly he opened his door and listened intently for a few moments. Hearing no movement, he stepped tentatively on to the cream carpet in the hall. Slowly he crept down the wooden staircase, keeping to the left to avoid loose floorboards. He hesitated every few steps to listen for movement on the landing. At the bottom of the steps, Jake breathed a sigh of relief. He seemed to be the only one awake.

Now in the downstairs hall, Jake didn't dither but headed straight for the sitting room. Light from the street streamed through the net curtains into the small room.

Jake walked towards the bay window. As he reached the sandy-colored sofa he knelt down and pushed it a few inches to the left. Yes! The carpet was loose there. He pulled up the corner and saw a small floor safe with a combination lock. Talk about security overkill.

Jake thought back to the afternoon. What *was* that security code? Oh yeah. He entered the numbers he remembered lifting from Emma's mind into the keypad. The lock whirred and clicked and he froze for a second. The sound too loud in the silent room.

Success! He moved a little to the left of the window to gain more light and opened the safe fully. It was filled with colored folders, which he stacked on the sofa arm one by one. Beneath them lay his parent's and, below it, another folder with his name.

He removed the two folders and carefully put everything back the way he'd found it and closed the safe. Silently, he moved the sofa back and tiptoed eagerly back up to his room.

Once in his bedroom, he kicked his dirty clothes across the floor and stuffed them against the crack under his door. Sure that no light would creep out into the landing, he turned his bedroom lamp on and tilted it to get maximum light on his bed. He sat down and looked at the two colored files.

The blue one bulged with something hard and solid. Jake emptied the contents over the duvet. An envelope, a crystal pendant and some loose paperwork spilled out. Ignoring the paperwork for now, Jake picked up the envelope. It was addressed to him in his dad's untidy scrawl. Underneath his name, he read that it was meant to be opened on his own eighteenth birthday. Taking the letter out of the yellowing envelope, he absent-mindedly smoothed the creases out of the paper.

His eyes roamed the page, scanning the type quickly, eager to know more.

Dear Jake,

First of all we want to say how proud we are of you, we love you and you will always be our son.

We couldn't find the words to tell you before but you were adopted when you were a baby. We will support you in every way we can if you want to look for your birth parents.

We included a pendant with this letter that was found with you. We should have given it to you years ago. Social Services insisted that we

> *had to because your birth parents wanted you to have it. We can only say we are sorry for not giving it to you before now but if we had we would have had to admit that you were adopted. We love you too much and thought we would lose you if we did that.*
>
> *We hope you can forgive us.*
>
> *Mum and Dad*

The paperwork looked like adoption documents. They had both his mother and father's signatures on them but no information about his real parents. The will in the last file only told him what he already knew - that in the event of his parents' death, his uncle, Ben, would look after him.

And there was the crystal.

It hung off a black leather thong, suspended in a circle of white metal. The crystal itself was small but clear. Holding it up to the light, he couldn't see any flaws. It looked like a perfect globe. Engraved on the edge of the metal, Jake could just make out some symbols, but these were far too small to see clearly.

Fascinated, Jake stared into the depths of the stone. In the lamplight, it glowed a soft yellow, green to blue and finally red and back to yellow from deep in the center. Feeling an irresistible urge to put it on, he slid it over his head and tucked it under his black t-shirt. A warmth began to emanate from the crystal, making him feel drowsy. As it crept though his body, Jake felt more relaxed than he'd ever felt before.

He lay back on to his pillows and closed his eyes. This was amazing, he felt like he was floating. His awareness expanded, taking in the whole room. He could see but he knew he had his eyes closed. Turning, he saw his body below him. Underneath the t-shirt there was a glow in the crack between the t-shirt and his skin. Wow.

This is weird, he thought. His legs hung off the bed at an odd angle while his upper body lay on his pillows. His arms were folded on his chest and obscured the logo underneath. However, his face seemed relaxed. He couldn't help comparing himself to his friend. Where Karl was relatively short and ginger, Jake was tall and blond. Jake grinned; he was taller than some of the teachers!

Thinking of school, he suddenly remembered

about his promise to meet Karl at the beach. Without warning he was floating towards the wall. Jake raised his arms over his eyes as the wall loomed closer. Of course, he didn't have arms! Silently yelling he passed through the bedroom wall. With horror, he felt rather than saw spiders scuttling in the wall and he was through to the outside. Taking a few seconds to gain his bearings he realized he was far from the ground. He was floating in mid-air! The realization hit him. *Oh my God, I'm floating in mid-air!* He told himself not to panic but vertigo began to set in. He began to fall. His thoughts froze as fear gripped his mind. The grass was getting closer but his friend filled his thoughts. He was supposed to be meeting Karl. What a time to be thinking of Karl! But he stopped falling and began to move along again. He was off, heading towards the sea.

As he floated, Jake became more confident. He tried to take in all the details. Everything was so clear. He'd always had good vision but he'd never seen anything like this! He could see the details of every brick of every house he passed.

He began to notice sounds and realized they were muted. A brown moth fluttered against a window across the road. His progress slowed as he concentrated on the insect and his hearing sharpened. Jake could hear the wings hitting the glass with a large regular thump, thump, thump. Suddenly, he began to hear other sounds. People were shouting in the house across the road and a baby was crying in another. A bat passed, the clicks a counterpoint to the other sounds. They were getting louder, Jake's instinct was to cover his ears, but he didn't have any hands. Karl. Karl he had to get to Karl. He was off again, the sounds muted once more.

Within moments he passed his school. It was dark now, its gates closed. It reminded him of a haunted house he'd seen from an old horror movie. He concentrated on the boy's wing and felt himself slow down. He circled over to Karl's window to see if he had already gone. The curtains were open and he saw two rows of beds. Jake looked to the left through the glazed windowpanes and sighed. He could tell from the shape on the bed that Karl had rolled up clothes to look like a person. *Matron should be wise to that trick by now. Maybe she didn't care?*

Thinking of people who didn't care, he was glad his uncle hadn't made him board here. He thought he might when he first arrived but Ben kept him at this school for appearance's sake. Fortunately for him, Ben hated spending more money than he had to on him. It was cramping his style. Paying for Jake to board there would mean he had less money to spend on his *girlfriends*. But again he wouldn't want his friends at the golf club to think he was mean so he was still allowed to be a day-boy - and Ben never let him forget it, Jake thought bitterly.

Jake recalled the will. When his parents died last year, Ben and Emma were left a third of their money. That was three hundred and fifty *thousand* pounds! It wasn't as if his parents had dumped him on them expecting them to struggle with him. The school fees didn't cost that much, he thought.

He could see the beach peeking through some trees; it wasn't too far now. This was the main reason everyone chose it as a meeting place. Following a break in the fence, a well-trodden mud path marked the way through the park. He was so close; he could see Karl's ginger hair shining like a beacon in the distant firelight. As usual he was sitting on the sand alone, slightly apart from everyone else. Jake felt a pang of guilt. It wasn't his fault. Karl would understand. After all, it wasn't every day you found out you were adopted or come to think of it left your body and flew!

Jake gently floated down to beach level and sat down next to his friend. A few of the others were standing next to the fire, chatting and drinking. Someone had brought some speakers and attached it to their phone and a few of the girls were dancing; a bottle in one hand and their phones in the other. Probably texting one another, Jake thought.

He turned to look at his friend; Karl had brought out one of his many books again. Craning to look at the cover, he could just make out *Existentialism from Dostoevsky to Sartre* in the firelight. His friend really needed to get a life. What was the point of going to these parties if he just read books? Jake sometimes despaired of his friend. All that scheming to be popular. Okay, they weren't popular - but they were invited. Surely, that was a step in the right direction.

Jake watched Karl put his book down to look at his watch. Jake jerked. Karl was staring straight at him! Jake twisted behind and realized that was the direction where he lived. As Jake looked back at his friend again he caught him shaking his head. Karl took out his mobile from his pocket. He swiped the screen to unlock it and pressed the green key.

Searching for Jake's number, he began to call.

Simultaneously, Jake could hear a ring in the distance. A sharp tug pulled him and he found himself hurtling back towards his body at an impossible speed. While before he had travelled around buildings now he went through them. Within seconds, he was back on his bed. Jake groaned, if he'd known that was going to happen he would have lain down properly! He leaned over to his bedside table exhausted. There was one missed call on his phone.

Jake rolled over to stare up at the ceiling. His mind was whirling; he needed to find out more about his real parents. Energized he sat up. Where could he find out more? Social Services! Jake sat down in front of his computer and tapped the spacebar on his keyboard. Moments later the familiar login screen lit his monitor. Thank God for Emma, he thought. She could be a pain but her need for a quiet life meant she'd do anything to get it. Not that I would ever take advantage, he smiled at the thought. Ben would never have let him have a computer without her insistence.

Using a search engine, Jake quickly found the public Social Services website. A quick search within the code found a link to the private site. *Don't you just love it when governments insist that everything is put online?* Jake grinned. *If it's on the web, I can get it.* Searching for the password-cracking program in his downloads folder, Jake's pendant started to glow imperceptibly. He opened one folder and closed it. Another, and another. Suddenly, hundreds of folders were opening and closing at an impossible rate as Jake looked for the file he needed. Another moment and Jake was *inside* the computer. It was so easy. It felt like he was in an incredibly large room with hundreds, even thousands of doors. All he had to do was just think of the door and it opened, think again and it closed. Easily finding the passcrack file on his computer in seconds he just applied the program to the website and he could sense millions of number combinations crashing against the security wall.

In just a few more minutes, he was in. Pausing to check there was no more security, he moved through to the adoption records. Another few moments and he found his name. Entering the folder, he visualized it as just another large room filled with paper suspended around him.

Grabbing the nearest, he found it was a newspaper clipping from the year he was found fourteen years ago. They had digitized the whole page. On the top was an advert and below it was a small picture of his adoptive parents holding a baby and a short description.

He was found at St Mary's, he read. He was a month to two months premature but miraculously healthy when a nurse found him abandoned on the steps. After a few months in an incubator, his new parents took him home.

He was found wrapped in a blanket with a crystal and a letter. Jake frowned, letter? What letter? Dropping the article, he grabbed the next few files; these were just progress reports for Social Services. He frowned and moved around the 'room' picking more up and discarding them again. It was all rubbish, where was the letter? In the 'corner' was another folder, only a few kilobytes large. Inside was a file labeled to be deleted.

Picking up the paper, eagerly he began to read. It was from his real mother. Just hours ago he would have thought it was all nonsense, but now... It said his name was Malo Omnax. Impatiently he skipped the next paragraph, something about being sorry.

He began to read more slowly with disbelief. There had been a coup in a place called Eleria? The Magi had killed the heads of four of the five great Elementi families, including the High-King his father, the letter explained. She had managed to escape and with the help of Ariel, the Air Queen, had sent him and the other children to Earth. She didn't know where the others went. The power was fading and all their systems were shut down to preserve energy. They had to use all the spare energy they had left to accelerate his growth so they could safely send him.

He had all four powers within him she said, fire, earth, air and water. With the crystal he had to find the other children and bring them back. Only together would they be able to defeat the Magi.

Wow, no wonder they marked this file for deletion. They must have thought she was a right nutcase. Thinking back though, it did make some sort of sense. He thought back to the beginning when he found he could make something catch fire just by thinking about it.

The first time had been an accident. He had lost his temper. Ben had promised that he would let him stay at Karl's but had said no at the last minute.

He'd been furious! How dare he. He wasn't even his father! Jake had stormed to his room, slamming the door behind him. The fury had built up, making him so mad, he felt like he would explode - and to his surprise the book in front of him burst into tall angry red flames. Luckily there had been half a glass of lemonade on his desk to put it out with. It was so cool.

After months of practice he found if he concentrated hard, so hard that every muscle in his body was tense, he could make something light up in front of him. It got easier the more he practiced. In fact it was how he got himself and Karl invited to the beach parties. His party trick was to light the bonfire... so that was fire. He could read minds - that had to be air. That only left earth and water.

Glancing around he decided he wouldn't be able to find out any more here, he was tired and it was getting late, he set the page in his hand to be printed on his computer.

About to leave, he halted. He had to do something about security. Jake found the door that led to the access logs on the server. Scanning them, he wiped all traces of his visit before jumping to a nearby proxy server. Making sure that it didn't keep any records of his visit, he jumped to a couple more servers before heading home.

Jake withdrew from the computer and sat back to stare at the blank screen. This was far too much to take in. He was a... No, not a magician; that was obviously what the Magi were. He picked up the printed letter. He was one of the Elementi - one of the rulers of Eleria with Talents. Not only that but he was a king - well he must be if he was the son of the High-King and he was dead. The spirit of the nation she had written. He looked down at the crystal. It had stopped glowing. It just looked like any other crystal he'd seen in jewelry shop windows down the high street.

Jake felt a wave of tiredness hit him. Exhausted, he looked at his clock. It was two in the morning. Turning the computer off, he lay back down on his bed. Clicking the light off, he turned to face the wall, closed his eyes and fell instantly asleep.

CHAPTER TWO
- MIRIM

Mirim opened her eyes, and sighed with contentment. Of all the islands on Eleria, this had to be the best. She smiled as she watched the boats bobbing on the horizon. Her visits to Pumar for fresh fruit and fish were always a welcome relief; she just wished there were more of them. It broke up yet another humdrum week. The vibrant port was so different compared to the white empty *soulless* Citadel.

Taking her cup, she found a seat along the edge of the covered stall area. The market wasn't fully open yet and she could see people at the red colored stalls nearest her were still setting up their fruit displays. The only stands serving customers were the grey fish booths nearer the cliff edge.

She had just enough time to sit down and unwind with a cup of dushu. Sipping with pleasure, she let the warm amber liquid soothe her parched throat. Closing her eyes again, she leant back against the woven chair and relaxed.

She let the islanders' thoughts sweep over her like a gentle breeze as she listened to their chatter. She loved the friendly banter among the stall owners and their customers. It reminded her of Byia, her friend from the next island along. They had been friends for years and had been inseparable once together. Each time her mother came to the market, they would sneak off to play for a couple of hours on the beach. A frown crossed Mirim's features as she remembered the last time she saw her friend. One day her mother had 'heard' her making plans to show her friend the entrance to the Citadel.

Mirim cringed at the memory. As soon as she'd decided to tell Byia, her mother had immediately sensed what she had been about to do. Within minutes, she had appeared like an avenging demon. Mirim relived the fear she felt when she spotted her mother approaching across the beach. Her mother had stalked up to them, the old queen's mouth set in a grim line, her mind clamped shut like a steel vice. She'd grabbed the seven-year-old Mirim's hand and dragged her across the sand. Mirim had never seen her mother so furious.

It was the first and only time the old Air Queen had used the air power on her daughter. Mirim had cried bitterly, tears running down her face. She wasn't really going to tell Byia she remembered arguing, but her mother knew different, she'd read the truth from her thoughts. Ignoring her cries, her mother mercilessly invaded her mind, slicing through her immature barriers with ease. She'd tried to resist but all she could do was let the tears fall down her cheeks as the compulsion grew in strength. She would never be able to talk about the Citadel's location.

Their trip ended there, and the old queen forbade her to see Byia again. They never went back to Yarn. Mirim could smile at the memory now but at the time she had screamed and sulked for days. Of course now she understood why her mother had done it. Her family had guarded the secret of the Citadel for almost a hundred years, ever since the Change. A child's temper tantrum could never be allowed to jeopardize that.

With her the old Air Queen gone, now it was

just her and the Matrix at the Citadel. Resolved to forget about it for just a few more minutes, Mirim relaxed and let her mind wander into the thoughts and dreams around her.

The islanders always seem so happy here, she thought wistfully. At that,, a shadow impinged on her awareness. She sat up slowly. Something was wrong, no, *different* - nearby. Trying not to draw attention to herself, she idly scanned the crowd. There were soldiers, here? Watching through half-shut eyes, she watched as two Arellian guards strode by.

Their facial tattoos weren't the only clue to their mercenary status even though they wore the standard uniform of the guard. Unusually, ugly blasters hung on their belts. They were remnants from the old Elementi Guard, she supposed. No one had the technology to create self-charging weapons any more. As mercenaries, they would easily be able to pay black market prices.

Their height was imposing, and they stood half a head taller than the island people. Tourists and islanders alike were trying not to stare at the conspicuous newcomers. Instinctively she probed into their public minds but found nothing useful. Their surface thoughts were unstructured, full of how they were too hot in their new uniforms, they were uncomfortable and - she smiled at this - how they could be earning far better pay hunting rebels, anywhere but here.

Mirim sighed. She would have to look deeper into their psyche. There must be a reason they were here. She was glad she had already eaten that morning; gods only knew what would be in there, she forced herself to look even further. Going past surface thoughts was always tiresome; the mind instinctively had defenses that had to be bypassed.

She struggled for a moment and sighed. It had to be done. This was the furthest you could get from any battleground she knew of, and they were clearly not here for the tourism. Sorting through the strands of thoughts around her, she looked deep into their minds.

Her body jerked, but at the curious looks from nearby stall owners, she leaned back again and pretended to bat away a fly. She had found what she needed.

From the memory of the nearest guard, she replayed the last briefing from his mind. She could see the old Elementi castle in Naven loom above the capital. Its imposing gray walls matched the rain-heavy clouds hovering in the distance. A passenger in the guard's memory,

Mirim could only watch through his eyes as he walked through the castle gates, through elaborately decorated corridors until he reached the Great Hall. Standing on a podium, she recognized the current Emperor-pretender's face from coins, Aras himself speaking to hundreds of mercenaries standing side by side facing the front as his voice boomed artificially through the room. He didn't look as though he was well. Sweat dripped from his forehead and his face looked haggard. Concentrating on his voice, she listened closely to his words. They had orders to find out what they could from the natives in the Empire. Aras was looking for the Citadel!

Mirim withdrew from the guard's mind gently, extricating her thoughts from his with the deft skill that only an air power had. Investigating further, Mirim stood up nonchalantly and sauntered along behind them. Careful to avoid notice, she began picking up the occasional piece of fruit. As she appeared to test its ripeness, she listened intently to the men.

The first stall owner was a Dikkar. He had never even heard of the Citadel. Even at the height of the Elementi Empire, the Citadel was a well-kept secret. His people were refugees from halfway around the globe. Although they had been one of the first people to fall under Aras' grandfather, they had still only reached the islands some sixty years ago.

The next couple of stall owners however were local. These admitted they had heard of it, but they thought it was in the other hemisphere. Satisfied, Mirim walked off towards the harbor. There was no point listening further. They didn't know anything.

A few hundred yards along the path she slipped behind some trees. Knowing her position was concealed from the soldiers and any prying eyes, she made herself invisible. Next, she cast her mind to create an image of herself for anyone who could be watching. Complete with a basket containing her market purchases, the image strolled onwards, towards one of the boats on the beach. To the casual observer she climbed into one of the small boats and began to row along the coast until it rounded a cliff, where she let the illusion drop. No wonder there were stories of ghost ships. She grinned. If anyone had been sitting at the headland...

Still behind the trees, Mirim walked on. Careful to be quiet, she headed along the cliff path towards a small grove. The locals regarded these trees as sacred. Something she and her family had cultivated over the last century. She knelt down by the largest of the trees, its broad branches protecting her fair skin from the morning sun. She took out a small yellow crystal from a silk pouch that hung around her neck.

Cautiously she scanned the area again for thoughts. Satisfied there were only birds and small animals present, she concentrated on the ground. The air around the foot of the tree shimmered to reveal a smooth metal hatch. Stooping, she lifted the hatch and climbed inside into the tunnel below.

Holding up her crystal again, she visualized the metal hatch above her. Concentrating hard, she pushed and pulled the air above with her power. The soil scraped back softly over the metal hatch and within seconds the tunnel was once again hidden from any visitors to the grove.

Mirim stood still for a few moments while her eyes adjusted to the new light. The walls emanated a low orange glow from rocks harvested from the sea. Hiking her basket over one shoulder, she began walking along the bare tunnel. Within half an hour, she was back in the Citadel.

Later that day, Mirim started to work on the maintenance she had neglected for weeks. She strode into the control room, expecting to see only the yellow crystals glowing. She stopped and frowned. Some lights on the control panel had activated. Only significant crystal power could make this happen. She ran forward. This can mean only one thing she thought with mounting excitement... one of the lost children must have activated his or her crystal!

Mirim reached into her pocket and her mind fused with her crystal with practiced ease. Using the energy she linked directly to the rudimentary mind of the crystal Matrix. As she did she felt it become sharper in response. She didn't understand how, but the Matrix bonded with humans, sharing their energy and somehow their intelligence. In return it had given certain families powers linked to crystals. Over time, those families were able to perform some feats without crystals, but with them they were immensely powerful. Those families were the Elementi.

When the five families were linked together through their crystals to the Matrix, the power was incredible - as was its intelligence. But, she thought sadly, it only has enough now to keep the data banks active. Over a thousand years of use generated only enough power to last a hundred years. It was now so drained that it relied on just her contact to keep the basic systems functional. It needed the Elementi back too.

With the combined intelligence, Mirim began to analyze the power logs of the outer crystals. Moving in a circular pattern, she could see that none of the secondary systems were used. The Earth, Fire and Water systems were clear. Her own element, air, showed her recent visit to the island.

With mounting excitement, she turned to the white crystals in the center. Mirim passed her crystal over the largest of the crystalline structures. These had been dead for almost a hundred years, but wait - a low hum and glow answered the lights from her own, smaller yellow stone.

Breathing quickly, she rechecked the logs. This could only mean one thing. The descendant of the High-King had to have used the Focic crystal. Remembering the instructions given by her mother, she accessed the main data banks. Using this she moved her mind through the main power conduits until she reached the battery hidden deep below the

Citadel. There was still enough power to make at least one return journey. Feeling exhilarated - this was what she had been waiting years for, she imagined a thin wiry yellow cord of light snaking out from the yellow section of the control panel to herself. She took one last look around the familiar spartan room and commanded the Matrix to send her to the last recorded place the ancient crystal had been used.

CHAPTER THREE - FIGHT

Mr. Galloway strode to the front of the class. Stopping he paused for effect and smartly turned by his desk to look at the clock on the far wall. His gaze scoured the room.

"Right, you can now turn your papers over, you have twenty minutes."

A rustle of papers filled the old classroom. Running his eyes down the paper, Jake glanced at Karl in alarm. A cold shiver of dread crawled down his back. This wasn't the periodic table. Karl looked back in dismay. As one they turned to look at Neil. The other boy's head rose from his copy of the test. He twisted to glare at them. He held his hand up and silently but slowly moved it across his neck. Karl swallowed nervously.

"You said it was the periodic tables!"

"It was, maybe he changed his mind." Jake whispered back.

Karl rubbed a hand through his hair, getting gel over it. Jake snorted.

"You won't be laughing when Neil gets us at break." Karl snapped back quietly, wiping his hands on his trousers.

As the test went on, Jake kept looking up at Neil only to find the other boy staring back, making slicing motions with his hand. It wasn't their fault. If Neil bothered to revise instead of using his mind reading! How was he supposed to know if a teacher decided to change a test after lessons? Karl didn't look up once. Then again, thought Jake, Karl could do that test standing on his head, a blindfold on with one arm tied up. They don't give scholarships to just anyone.

It was the longest twenty minutes of Jake's life. Mr. Galloway strolled up and down the room but he wouldn't be around during break. Jake began to gulp convulsively. Ten minutes to go. How were they going to get out of this one? Karl kicked out and hit his shin without looking up. Jake shook himself, nursing his leg. Right, test now, panic later. He bent down to his paper again.

As the bell rang for the end of lesson, Jake's heart began to beat rapidly as he tensed to run. The chairs scraped back loudly and everyone ran to the door. Jake and Karl were in the lead.

"What are we going to do?" Karl panted.

"Get out of here. We need to find somewhere to hide... Fast!"

They raced out into the quadrangle. As they reached the center, Jake twisted to look behind him; Neil was weaving his way through, pushing people out of the way. Jake circled frantically on the spot, looking for somewhere to go. The play area was bare, but the teachers wouldn't allow them to go back inside. There was only one place to go.

Jake grabbed Karl, causing him to yelp as he almost dislocated his shoulder.

"Watch out!"

"Come *on*!"

Maybe if they hid behind the bins. They changed direction at the last moment and dived behind the recycling bins. Karl looked around.

"I hate to burst your bubble, Jake, but there's nowhere to hide here either." Karl muttered.

Jake bit his lip, big mistake.

"Do you think I'm an idiot?" Neil's voice drifted from behind them. Jake whirled around.

"Don't" Jake warned Karl. Cringing inside he knew his friend wouldn't be able to resist that one.

"We don't think you're an idiot at all..."

Neil's fist unclenched slightly.

"...but who would we be to disagree with everyone else?"

Of course now, Jake thought bitterly, now we need them, there are no teachers around.

Neil did not even bother to retort. His hands shaped into fists by his side and he strode up to them. Jake grabbed Karl and pushed his friend behind him. Karl tried to push in front but Jake knew he was no match for Neil.

Neil threw a punch at Jake. Time seemed to slow to crawl. Jake was strangely fascinated by how Neil's face twisted as he grunted with the effort as he moved. The boy's face screwed up with concentration and hate, and suddenly the spell was broken. Jake panicked. He had to defend himself!

As Neil pulled back his arm, readying his punch, Jake felt a gentle warmth as the crystal started to glow under his school shirt. He felt stronger, more confident. At the same time, Jakes' thoughts raced, faster than he thought possible, and he wished he had a shield. A picture of the Viking shield he had seen at the re-enactment two weeks ago flashed in his mind. Neil's hand loomed inches from his face. Jake flinched, if only he had taken up Judo, Karate even wrestling - anything, instead of play sword fighting! Neil's fist filled his vision. There was no time to duck. Jake closed his eyes in silent prayer. How he wished he had that shield! A jolt of electricity coursed through his body and a transparent barrier made of air formed in front of Jake's face. Neil's hand smashed into the wall of air. There was a loud crack followed by Neil's howl of pain.

Jake didn't realize how badly Neil was hurt and reached with his mind and called for something, anything to help him. Neil was not only tall, but his father owned a gym and he was very strong. He would easily beat him up if he were given a chance.

The ground began to shake. The force increased in tandem with his panic. Karl stood behind Jake and stared wildly about them. As Karl was distracted, a spurt of dirty water arced from a drain behind Neil hitting the bully full in the back of the head. Neil dropped like a stone. In the moment it took to happen - Karl missed it.

"Did you feel that? That had to be an earthquake!" Karl exclaimed. Suddenly he noticed Neil on the floor, he grabbed Jake.

"H-h-how did... What have you done? Quick, we need to leave before any teachers get here. This'll mean a detention for sure."

CHAPTER FOUR - DESTINY

Mirim gasped, disorientated. She knew it would only last a few seconds but the nausea always lasted that moment more than she expected. Leaning against the nearest tree, she tried to regain her bearings. As the feeling passed, she was able to see her surroundings better.

So this is Earth. Mirim knew this was the last place the Matrix had detected power use. This has to be where he lives, she thought. Standing on the pavement she looked down the street. On each side of the road, there were rows of well-kept three-story houses. Knowing the Matrix would have sent her to the nearest point, she guessed the house beside her on the right had to be it.

She let go of the tree to take a closer look. A

six-foot hedge surrounded the house. An ornate wrought iron gate marked the main entrance to the property and from this she could see a small driveway leading up to the main house. A large oak tree obscured the top two windows on the right side of the building. Beside the main entrance, there was a small metal box. Moving closer she saw that it was a communications device. She guessed pressing the button would allow her to talk to the inhabitants.

Removing her crystal from its pouch round her neck again, she concentrated on its depths. Spreading her awareness towards the house, she scanned for life. Apart from one small animal, there was no one home.

Now she had two choices she reflected - remain here for the new High-King to return or wait for him to use his powers again and go to him. Deciding to take the latter choice, she sat down. Time was important, once activated it was impossible to resist using the crystals again, especially when the new boy-king would not be trained in its use.

Needing to find out more about this strange place, Mirim looked deep into her crystal. Losing herself once again in its yellow depths, she directed the building energy to the primitive cable above her head. She needed to find the nearest information source.

Literally in her element, Mirim used her talent to sort out the streams of data flying through the air to find what she was looking for. She grew excited as she began to recognize patterns. There was a network almost like the Matrix here! A computer connected wirelessly from a nearby house was an easy access point to a huge data bank of information. Using this she first downloaded all the information from its hard drive before tapping the net in search of more information about the culture.

The stream of information was far too much, but connected to the Matrix in Eleria, no matter how tenuous the link, Mirim was able to send it back through the yellow psychic cord emanating from the back of her mind. The Matrix received the information and stored it, making it available in smaller, more manageable chunks for her when she needed it.

Her people's knowledge of this world had always been rudimentary at best. The data banks of the Matrix previously had only held the most basic information - that no mind or crystal power was used here. Back before the Change, the technological development recorded on Earth was not advanced but that was a hundred years ago.

The thought mulled in her mind - it had been dangerous sending them here. Her people didn't know anything about this culture. A hundred years ago, it would have been a very different place. She knew that even though they could send the children a hundred years into the future to here, her ancestors could only 'see' the time frame they were in. Life had changed so much in that time. It had been a risk.

Still connected to the computer, she searched for pictures of people. Most wore mostly blue trousers and short, finely woven tops. Well, if so many were wearing them, these must be what she should be wearing to avoid standing out. Her lip curled, some of the other outfits were far too revealing for her taste.

Mirim took out a high calorie snack from the pocket of her yellow skirt. It seemed an age since she had last eaten and she was not fond of nut bars. Still, it was the best source of energy for what she was about to do. She took a bite and felt the energy revive her.

Taking an image from the many she had seen she began to change the structure of the clothing she wore. She didn't see the white lace top and bright yellow skirt she had put on to go to the island but instead she saw a sea of vibrating atoms. Manipulating them, she applied the image to her outfit. There was a brief flash of light and excess heat dispersed to reveal her new clothes.

Happy with the new look, Mirim felt the coarse woven material of the blue trousers. She supposed it would be hard wearing but was pleased with the feel of the short-sleeved yellow top. Mirim again turned to the network of information and searched for their current technological level. Deep in an article on computers, she marveled at how different their technologies were. A hundred years ago, Eleria was far superior in technology to here, but now... Aras' family had done far more damage to their civilization than she had even suspected. Reaching the end of the article, she felt a powerful surge of power shimmer the air around her. Quickly she requested the location of the source from the Matrix.

Alert, she realized that if she knew the High-King was alive and was now active, others would not be far behind. Mirim cast about with her mind, pulling strands of energy from all directions around her. When she sensed she had enough, she concentrated on the coordinates the Matrix sent her. Her vision blurred as her surroundings morphed into the immediate area of the source of the surge.

Fighting the nausea that always followed teleportation, Mirim scanned the data banks for information on the building in front of her. It seemed this was a place of learning. There were only certain circumstances that she would be able to take the boy out but first she had to find out his name. Again connecting through the cables above, she was able to access the school computer system easily. She almost felt contemptuous of the security measures she met. Using the street name she had first teleported to, she searched through the list until only one pupil matched her search - Jake Richards.

Mirim looked deeper into the records. His parents were dead. They died last year in a car crash. He had no siblings. There would be no real ties to this place for him. His guardians were Ben, his father's brother and his wife Emma, who worked for the local government. Mirim nodded. It was all perfect.

Back on the Internet Mirim quickly found the local government website. Eventually finding a picture of Emma Richards, she smiled. *Excellent; time for an illusion.*

****

A few yards down the road, an old lady sat patiently waiting at a bus shelter. Bored and uncomfortable on the hard plastic seats, her gaze wandered aimlessly. Idly looking across at the old private school in front of her she spotted a young woman dressed in jeans and a sunflower yellow t-shirt vacantly staring at the brick wall surrounding the school. Curious, the old lady watched the younger woman as her features gradually morphed. As the psychic field reached the old lady she saw the girl change shape. Her long blonde hair shriveled to make a neat bob, its color darkened to become a dark chestnut brown, almost black. Her cheeks became plumper, while her lips thinned. The jeans and t-shirt blurred to become a calf-length green dress. The woman gasped. The girl twisted to look at the startled old lady and grinned. Patting the creases on her dress, she walked through the gates of the school.

****

A short driveway led up to the main school and the first door she tried opened into a reception area. A young chatty receptionist with a ready smile greeted Mirim as she stepped in.

"Mrs. Richards? We haven't seen you in a while, have you come to pick-up Jake? He's in the Headmaster's office at the moment. He's been in a fight, I'm afraid." Without waiting for a response the receptionist continued. Her voice turned quizzical. "I didn't realize the Headmaster had phoned you himself."

Further up the hall, the door to the headmaster's office opened and Jake walked out in a daze.

"Good timing." said the receptionist turning to her computer.

Mirim tentatively reached out to sense his thoughts. She had to be careful. As the son of the last High-King, he would have the powers of the air element as well as the others. He would easily be able to sense her intrusion if she wasn't discreet. Luckily he was too wrapped up in something that had just happened.

Mirim watched the drama unfold in Jake's mind. So that was the source of the power use. *Great timing indeed,* she thought. *I couldn't have planned it better.* Striding up to Jake, she took his hand and walked him outside. Still lost in his own thoughts he didn't notice something wasn't right about his guardian - or even that it was strange she had come to pick him up.

They stopped at the corner down the street

and Mirim turned to look fully into Jake's eyes. Making sure that he could see her clearly, she began little by little to drop her disguise. Jake gasped. Her hair was growing, her face thinned... she was getting younger! There was something eerily familiar about her, but he didn't recognize her. Jake snatched his arm back. It felt like something in him was tugging towards her, telling him that she was to be trusted... but another part was screaming that he didn't know her. She could be anyone. His world changed in an instant.

"Who are you?" he asked.

"My name is Mirim Ariel. I've come to take you home."

CHAPTER FIVE - ARAS

"My Lord, the healer is here," the attendant announced. She quietly ushered through a gray-robed man into the chamber. Once they reached the front of the dais, she moved back into position beside Aras.

Through the agony of another migraine, the young Emperor watched the other man approach. Aras cursed. The man had to be another fake. He was gratified to feel fear in the other man's mind.

Turning to his attendant, he said gruffly "Has he been told everything?"

"Yes my Lord." The servant whispered back. "He knows to make as little sound as possible during the ceremony."

Relieved, Aras nodded at the visiting wizard

to continue. Aras plucked the man's name easily from his mind. Ecu bowed in response and drew back his hood to reveal hawk-like features, with dark close-set eyes, under heavy brows with a nose too prominent, Aras' thought uncharitably.

The man's mouth set in a grim line as he silently drew a wide chalk circle on the marble floor. Careful not to smudge the chalk, he began to put his equipment into precise positions within its confines in front of the dais.

First, he placed a bowl of oil in the center. This was set on a tripod representing birth, death and life - Magi magic.

Aras relaxed, settling back in his chair. He was familiar with this. Next the man surrounded the tripod with objects in a circle to represent the elements; a feather for air, moss for earth, a lit candle for fire and a small vial of water.

Aras glanced at Ecu for an explanation.

"Your power is from two sources, my Lord. As you know, one is from your great-grandmother who gave you the undiluted power of the Magi, and the other from the Elementi. Your powers are disharmonious. One is fighting the other.

"These two forms of power should never be combined in one man. Your great-grandmother did something admirable.

However, by tricking the last High-King and bearing his child, she created something against the forces of nature. You can command both forms of magic but it was at a price."

"I know this!" Aras snapped. He winced at the pain the outburst cost him.

"My Lord, as your Magi power is corrupted, I must use a corrupted magic to find out why you are being affected this way. Why now? I understand from the attendant beside you that usually you only suffer mild headaches and that you have been able to live a normal life until now.

"It is my belief," Ecu continued, he looked even more nervous, "that your inheritance of these powers can only lead to a premature death. However, something has happened recently to hasten this. I need to use the tripod to ascertain what has happened. The spirits that guide me cannot only look into this world but can seek through the veil into other dimensions as well."

This was new. Aras hadn't been told of these places before. He leaned forward in interest.

"Dimensions?"

"Sire, I have reason to believe that your grandmother was not able to slay all of the Elementi. Records at the Great Library indicate the bodies of the High-Queen and one of the lesser queens were never found. Furthermore, the children were also never found. She thought they were destroyed in the Winter Palace fire, but..."

He broke off as he nervously fiddled with the collar of his robe.

"There is a possibility that the Elementi may rise again. With another High-King and a representative from each of the other four families, your throne may be in danger."

Aras looked skeptically at the old man. "The old king died without issue, except for my grandfather - my great-grandmother made sure of that! Still, you have my interest; continue."

Ecu finally had the objects to his satisfaction. He stepped into the center of the circle beside the tripod. As he stirred the oil, a putrid fragrance rose from the bowl that swamped the sweet smell from the lit candle nearby. As he breathed in the odor, Ecu's eyes rolled back to leave a milky mist in their place. The courtiers' clothes rustled as they craned forward to see more.

Ecu's body began to shake as the Magi and Elemental magics fought for dominance. To keep them in check, he laid his hands over the bowl, muttering words that neither the surrounding servants nor Aras could hear clearly. The objects in the outer circle began to glow and slowly rise.

The smoke swirled over the bowl and spilled to fill the circle. Aras could just make out the objects representing the elements spinning haphazardly inside the vapor. The smoke gradually coalesced to form a thick dense sheet over the bowl. The floating objects slowly sank to the ground. Images emerged against the grey background at an incredible speed. "Show me the source of the king's pain," cried Ecu. The images slowed down, forming and reforming until finally, a small room appeared.

Aras leaned forward. The wall of smoke towered over Ecu. It was the breadth of five hand spans wide and around two finger-widths deep, he reckoned. The images shown within were incredibly clear. Standing up with difficulty, Aras walked around the outside of the spelled circle. The steam from the oil swirled in the upright oblong with the picture overlaid. Aras could see the same image from all directions. He stumbled back to sit on the throne.

The room in the smoke held a bed, a table to the side of the room with a small narrow box on the top and a larger square box beneath. There was a boy lying on the bed. Moving closer again, Aras' breath caught in his throat.

The boy could have been his twin - only a few years younger. The boy was young, obviously. He could be only fourteen - sixteen at the most. He was tall, had the same blond hair only lighter and... His eyes narrowed - he had a crystal. Aras could just make out the glow from under the boy's clothing. This was impossible, but he was there. How could he exist?

The old man's eyes cleared. As they did, the smoke evaporated along with the picture.

Aras looked at the faces of the courtiers standing around; they did not seem to have grasped the full import yet.

"Out," he snapped.

"Lord?" replied a dignitary. He quailed as Aras turned to look at him.

"You dare to question me?"

Standing quietly to the side the First Advisor stepped forward and grabbed the young boy roughly by the collar of his tunic.

"You heard him, everyone out." He shoved the boy towards the door. The room shuffled to the exit. Satisfied the room was emptying, the first Advisor moved back to stand once again beside Aras.

Aras looked at him sharply.

"You too," he said quietly

"But Sire, you don't know this man."

Aras's headache throbbed, his temper rose to breaking point.

"Get out now, or all your years of service will not save you."

His tone brooked no argument. The Adviser's face drained of all color. He took a step backwards and left glancing back at Aras and the stranger with speculation in his eyes.

 Exhausted but watching the Advisor leave with interest, Ecu asked, "When did your headaches begin at the level you have them now?"

Aras looked thoughtful "Only a couple of days ago."

"That is when the crystal was first used. It would seem the High-Queen was pregnant when she escaped. If you want the headaches to disappear you will need to eliminate the boy. If not to save the Empire your great-grandmother founded, you must do it to save yourself!"

Ecu paused to emphasize his point, "that boy is the true heir. His families have been prepared for the power of the Matrix for generations. His blood is not only pure, but the Matrix must have accepted him before being sent to safety. Without him the Matrix may be persuaded to accept you. The scrolls say the Matrix needs a human mind to be sentient and for true sentience it needs to bond with a Spirit Elemental. While he is alive the Matrix, even buried in the Citadel will know this and you will never gain the full power of the Elementi."

"Citadel, what Citadel?"

"Did you think the fabulous power of the Elementi were from those small crystals they carried around their necks? In part, that is truth, but from my research, these were just conduits to the power of the Citadel.

"Your great-grandmother did not know this or she would not have been so quick to have killed the Elementi without first obtaining its location."

"Do you know the location of the Citadel?" Aras asked.

"Sadly not." Ecu shook his head. "I do know that it was built near the location where the first settlers arrived here. Legend has it that explorers found themselves in a crystal cave. Five of their number were somehow... changed. They became the Elementi - half of your ancestors. As you know our race came to Eleria later."

Aras leant back against the chair, trying to block out the pain. "This is all very interesting, but all I can think of at the moment is this pain!" Bored with the audience he scanned Ecu's mind for all the information he had on the Matrix. There wasn't much but it was enough to think about.

"My Lord, I am sorry." Contrite, carefully stepping out of the circle, Ecu moved to give the young Emperor some tablets he took out of his robe. Guards at either side leaped forward to block his access.

"My Lord, you need only take this medication I have distilled from some herbs and it will abate the pain for a couple of hours. They will help until another remedy can be found." He offered the tablets.

The guard on his left reached out to pull on a silken chord suspended from a bronze frame. A bell sounded in the distance. Moments later the attendant who ushered Ecu to the room earlier, quietly stole in. The guard nodded at the tablets. She took them and swallowed one. Everyone froze in a still tableaux waiting for a reaction. Seeing none, Aras nodded at the guards. They stepped back into position. The attendant passed the remaining tablets to Aras.

"Do you have any more?" Aras asked.

"I need only a workroom and a few hours to make more, my Lord."

A young girl, sitting quietly in the corner stood up. Reaching for a glass on the gold table beside her, she carried it over to Aras. Grimly, he took the glass and swallowed the pill. Everyone in the room from courtier to servant tensed, praying that this time it would work. Five minutes passed before Aras' face calmed showing the pain receding. As one, everyone in the room visibly relaxed.

Aras, stood up, "Ecu! You are a good man to have around. Please stay for a while. Marta will show you to one of the guest-rooms with enough space that you can make the tablets and more."

"My Lord, you are too generous." Ecu bowed and followed the attendant out of the room.

Entering the corridor, Ecu and Marta walked in silence for a moment. When they turned the first corner, Ecu whispered conspiratorially to Marta, "Who was the girl?"

Marta eyes appraised him for a few moments before replying.

"That was Shenella. They have been grooming her to become the next Empress. She was against the idea to start with but I hear her family soon beat her out of that notion. I suppose she knows whatever child she has will suffer the same fate as Aras." She added conspiratorially, "To be honest it is better to be the power behind the throne. Consorts do not last long with that family."

Ecu thoughtfully stroked his red beard. "Indeed, with a good adviser and a good woman, who knows what can be achieved?"

Marta giggled. "I see we are in agreement. I am already one of his favorites. By the by, do you have a potion or spell which could cement this?"

"You are his favorite, yet he still chose you to test the pill?"

"He trusts no one. I am as much a favorite as much as anyone can be."

"What about the girl?"

"It would be better to be his love than his wife, she is welcome to him," she said derisively. "What did you mean that he would not live long in there?"

"With just one source of magic, he would live a long life, indeed with our magic - a longer life than most. The Elementi use a natural source of power. They are incompatible, theirs is fighting ours, curtailing it. Every time he uses it he loses a few years."

"But, I haven't seen any evidence of him using

the crystal power. He doesn't even *possess* a crystal."

"He's been using it whether he knows it or not. Every time he unintentionally reads another's thoughts, or even when the other boy uses his powers. They are linked. There can only be one High-King, one of the spirit." At her blank look, he explained. "The white crystal, he instinctively draws power from the Matrix, all be it weakly. His body is not strong enough to withhold that sort of energy - as well as Magi power.

"Aras should not exist at all, but a small part of the power resides in him nevertheless. As the other boy gets stronger, so does the Elementi power - this weakens Aras and with it our chances to rule through him."

Searching through his robe, Ecu pulled out an elegant ruby ring. Pressing lightly on either side, the ruby popped up on a hidden hinge. Within, she saw a small amount of white powder. "Find a way to mix this in a drink and he will fall in love with the first person he sees."

"You just happened to have that in your pocket?"

He grinned, "I have a certain amount of precognition my dear. It has come in quite handy over the years."

Marta nodded without understanding and pushed open an ornate door with a fountain engraved on the wood. Ecu raised an enquiring brow at Marta.

"This suite used to belong to the Water King and his consort," she explained. "I thought if you were going to be important you should be given one of the more prestigious rooms."

In the throne room Aras realized he felt better. As he mulled over what his new adviser told him, he decided to take action. He needed to 'eliminate' the boy king before he got any stronger but also find that Citadel. The boy was obviously just finding out about his power or he would have got ill sooner. First, the Citadel.

"Get the new guards," he called.

Within moments the new batch of mercenaries filed into the room. A few days with his generals and they made credible guards but Aras could only feel contempt for these men. Their loyalties went to the highest bidder. Fortunately for him with the Elementi treasure stolen over a hundred years ago, he *was* the richest bidder around - barring his Magi cousins across the water..

Still, the men wore his uniform well, he thought with pride. There were at least a couple of hundred recruits all wearing the royal insignia. He could tell they were not comfortable with it. Aras didn't care; he needed them to display his emblem. The more his power was visible in the streets, the better his hold of it was. The black trousers and shirts were also ideal for missions where his soldiers needed to be inconspicuous at night. For those who saw it, the silver moon and pentagrams on the back of each shirt caused disquiet among watching foe and friend alike. Another good thing about mercenaries over his own guard, he mused was that they obeyed his orders flawlessly - without question. They had no conscience and were usually brighter than the usual soldier. Stupid mercenaries didn't last long.

Within minutes, Aras had given his commands to the generals in the front and although the men could hear them, the generals in turn informed the mercenaries standing in line behind them. Rows of men stamped their feet on the ground and turned smartly leaving the room on their first mission. Someone out there had to know where the Citadel was.

Task accomplished, Aras turned to the next. With trepidation he rose from the throne. It was always dangerous dealing with spirits and his command of his magic over the last couple of days had not been as good as it could have been.

Aras waived his attendants away and walked to the opposite side of the Great Hall, He entered a small anteroom off the throne room, where a secret room built by his grandfather was hidden. He locked the door behind him, muttering a quick lock spell for good measure. He stepped across to the opposite wall.

Reaching for the second torch bracket from the corner, Aras pressed a stud to the side of it. A tall mirror to his right swung inwards. His gaunt expression in the reflection caught him by surprise, Aras realized the tablets would only last for two hours before the pain would come back. He needed to hurry.

This room was a lot darker than the previous one. Aras muttered "incendi" and the room lit with a dull glow. All the walls and ceiling were black. A cursory glance upwards revealed the perfect reproduction of the night sky painted on the ceiling.

When still a child his father had told him about its construction. The artist who had created it was promised riches beyond his wildest dreams but at the last brush stroke he was killed as had the workmen who had partitioned the room off - as had the magician who had spelled the painting afterwards.

The sky was not only a perfect representation but also it stayed that way. As the world orbited the sun, the painting changed to show the new celestial sky without the inconvenience of clouds.

In the center of the room lay a painted white circle. Aras paused at the reminder. There were burn marks inside it. Shuddering, he composed his mind. This was dangerous. Taking slow breaths he drew in and focused his magic. When he felt he had enough he began to summon a Deoc.

The room began to smell of sulfur as the being he called fought for its freedom. Sweat broke out on Aras' forehead. His body felt like it was on fire. This was a strong one, or did it show how much he had been weakened by the rise of the Elementi power? An acrid stench filled his nostrils, but he held on. Throwing the last of his energy in, he felt the creature's presence fill the room.

In the circle, the Deoc glared at Aras. Its body was made entirely of fire but as Aras watched, the flames flickered and died out. Skin formed over the creature's body, first on its arms and legs. At last its face formed, and it was covered completely in skin. Over this, a robe appeared until a man stood before him with red and gold-flecked eyes.

"What do you want?"

"I need you to kill a boy."

"Why would I do that?" The creature smiled, confident in its power.

"You have no choice."

Testing his strength, Aras felt the creature try to find a chink in his defenses. Finding an impenetrable wall, the thing conceded. "Who and where is the boy?"

"The boy is in another dimension. The high Elementi sent the boy to safety where I cannot follow. You on the other hand are a creature from beyond the veil - you can."

Contemptuously, the creature smirked, "I cannot do this without more information. I am not a god!"

"He has the Elementi Spirit power. This means he has all the four powers in small measure so that he has the ability to focus the combined power of all the families. I too have that power. You can use mine to scent him out. He looks like this..."

An image of the room Aras had seen earlier in the smoke appeared in front of them. "Why me? Cannot one of your own magicians traverse the boundary?"

"They can, but I need you to get close to the boy. The new High-King will have to reunite the powers. He might be able to tell if any person I send is an impostor. Our magic is opposite. We use the spirits and illusion while they use natural magic. You, on the other hand, can pretend to be the fire element. Fire is natural to you as using fire would be to the real fire king or queen.

"Furthermore, I need you to find out where the Citadel is. With this, I would have almost limitless power. I would be able to control the Elementi side of my inheritance and combine the power of the Magi with it. Together I could control the world without the need to fight the battles one by one. Within hours, I could have complete control of the entire world and there would be no one and nothing that could stop me. Not the Matrix and not even my cousins in the Magi Empire."

"You are mad, human!"

"I may be mad, but you still have to obey me!"

"As you will."

The creature gave a mocking bow. It realized

the task might be more profitable than he at first thought. This human was stupid. If he could find out the location of the Citadel, what would stop him taking it over? He was the fire element incarnate. He stared at Aras, taking in his form, his essence, noting the dark stream of magic running through his blood. Entwined with it was the glittering white power of the Elementi, wrapping around getting stronger as the boy lived. The Elementi power was still the same strength as the Magi he observed. How long before the Elementi side took over and tried to destroy the unnatural Magi? Enough! It was not his problem. He had the scent. It was now time to find that boy!

The spell dropped and Adramelech exploded away. For a moment he stood still between dimensions. He discarded the human shape he had taken to communicate with Aras, returning to his natural fire-form.

Silent, in the darkness he quieted his mind, gently rotating trying to find the trail. Moving slowly now, he searched for the white thread meticulously. After a few moments he saw it, faraway, shining brightly in the complete darkness between worlds. How could he have missed that? As he drew closer it grew brighter and clearer. Whoever had sent the boy out of

Eleria had sent him to the future as well. The trail was as fresh as if the boy was sent only a few years ago. In effect, he had. Following the cord, the creature burst into the other reality.

CHAPTER SIX
- IRELAND

Men in hard hats watched as another caravan invaded their construction site. Hands in pockets, they stood in clusters by the main entrance, they could barely disguise the hatred that marred their normally jovial features. Some idiot had forgotten to lock the gates last night. It didn't matter how quickly they could get rid of them, work would be delayed for at least a week, most likely more. They wouldn't get paid for waiting - not on their contracts. There would be recriminations all round, even the union couldn't help with this one.

Inside the compound one of the new inhabitants, Kiera, stared defiantly back at them. What did these people expect? We have to stop somewhere! Here was as good as anywhere else. Turning away bored, she picked up the washing she had taken down from the line she had put up only the night before. They were here now and the locals had better get used to it.

She carried the washing into the caravan she shared with her father. Luckily, he was out, so after dumping it on the table, she went straight to her room. Kiera sprawled on the bed and looked up at the ceiling. The caravan was such a difference to the tent they had slept in just a few years ago. It had been the traditional way of life, but she didn't miss it. Now her father had come into some money he had bought the best mobile home in Ireland that could be found.

Kiera reached out to stroke the long green strands of the spider plant in the window. She marveled at their change of circumstances. She hated doing what she had to do, but she had to admit it was profitable. Still, it was only a matter of time before the Garda caught on. They had been lucky so far.

It really was time to move on. Her face twisted with distress, "I hate the city!" She let the despair wash over her. What was the use? Her father insisted they go there. It was better pickings he said and it was a lot easier to hide in. She remembered the first time her father had realized she had abilities. When he'd finally found out she could sense the differences between precious metals and stones.

She couldn't remember her exact age when Aunt Clara had shown her the box of her old jewelry, but she couldn't have been any older than seven. Her aunt had shown her what each gem was. She was surprised and pleased at how quickly Kiera picked it up. For Kiera though, it was easy to tell them apart. They not only looked different but they *felt* different. It was as if they resonated on a different frequency. Even if they were a different color she knew what they were immediately. She knew what their essence was. She just needed to be shown one example of a type.

Impressed, her aunt had told her friends. Soon all the women in their camp had brought their jewelry to find out what they had. She was able to guess what they were and after a while she was also able to let them know how much they were worth. Her aunt charged them a small amount but it was at least enough to buy books. With them she was able to teach Kiera how to read and write in secret.

Aunt Clara was not really one of the travelers but had fallen in love with her father's brother and never left. Kiera had loved to hear the story growing up, it was so romantic, but she wasn't one of them. Kiera's father would never have approved of her teaching his daughter.

Her aunt had managed to keep Kiera's skills a secret for longer than she thought possible - only the women had known, and for at least a year. Aunt Clara knew Kiera's father only too well. That was until he arrived home early one day.

Kiera remembered his face as he had walked in to Aunt Clara's caravan - stony.

"I've been looking all over for you. What are you doing?" he'd asked. Not realizing anything was wrong; the old lady sitting opposite Kiera told him that Kiera was valuing her jewelry for her. Kiera's heart dropped. What would he do?

To Kiera's relief, he acted casual. The stupid woman had warbled on obliviously.

"It's amazing," the lady said, "you must be very proud. I don't know anyone else who can value a stone without even looking at it!" Kiera could tell this infuriated him. Small red dots of anger appeared on his cheeks... but still he managed to keep his rage in check. He just nodded, his eyes flickered briefly and then he stalked away.

She thought he'd forgotten about it. For days

he made no mention of it. As usual she made breakfast for both of them on the open fire and each morning he went out, returning in the early hours.

It wasn't her father's fault, she reflected. He just wasn't any good at adapting to change. He used to be a tinsmith her aunt had told her. They didn't need much and he had made a respectable amount of money - enough so they could live on it - until plastics became ubiquitous. This was before Kiera could remember, but she was told he was a different man.

As it got harder and harder to travel and more difficult to sell his skills, he became bitter. It was their right to travel, he kept insisting, and Kiera could tell it was only a matter of time before he exploded. Every year more campsites were taken away, and every year a small part of his heart was turned to ice.

...*And that is where I came in,* she thought. That evening he returned home, but this time with a stranger. It wasn't like any traveler Kiera had seen before. To Kiera he was big, not tall. He wasn't fat, but he had to be the largest man she had ever seen.

She watched as they talked at the campfire. As she approached they quieted as she served them coffee in tin mugs, chatting animatedly again when she withdrew to the other side of the fire.

Through the crackling flames she studied his features. The stranger had a scar running from the corner of his left eye, along his cheek to the lobe of his ear. It must have healed wrong she thought. Whatever happened to him happened recently and had left that vivid purple mark. Although she tried, she couldn't help staring at it. As she watched she grew nervous, they were talking about her - her father kept pointing in her direction across the fire and gesturing excitedly at the man.

Kiera shivered with apprehension, wrapping her arms about herself. Trying hard to lip-read, she found it very difficult to understand what was going on. Without warning their voices became clearer. It sounded like they were seated right next to her. Her father explained what she could do. Tingles of fear trickled down her back and despite the fire, she felt cold. The man seemed very interested but hope rose as he seemed skeptical.

She could almost swear that she heard more than they were actually saying. It was impossible but she knew that if she couldn't to do what they would ask her, that man would happily kill her father - for wasting his time just as easily as if she just refused to do it.

They wanted to test her first, so the first job had been easy. They were checking to see if what her father had said was true. They picked her up the following night when the rest of the camp was asleep. It was too dark to read the number plate or even see the color of the car clearly, but she suspected that they would not be the real plates anyway.

There were four men already in the car. She squeezed into the remaining space in the back. They all wore black suits and looked like bouncers she'd once seen in Dublin. The cramped two-hour drive was excruciating - no one spoke, not even to introduce themselves.

She had no idea where they were going and she wasn't told what to expect. When grilled about the journey later by her father she could only describe the outside of the house they had arrived at. For all she knew they had been driving in circles for the two hours she was gone.

They pulled up outside a large detached town house, passing a Ferrari shining silver-grey in the moonlight. Three men got out quietly and signaled for her to follow them. At the door she was surprised to find that they already had a key. The tallest man fitted the key in the lock but it didn't work. Unperturbed he tried another similar key from the ring. It wasn't until the third key the door opened. Everyone piled inside, eager to get away from any prying eyes. One of the men spoke in a whisper.

"Right, Campbell said you were good. The owners have gone on holiday for a week but we still have to be quiet. There should be some diamonds here. Can you find them?"

Kiera frowned. Standing still, she let her awareness gradually spread out from her body, seeking that special resonance that only a diamond has. There was nothing on the ground floor. Climbing the staircase she let her awareness spread out further as she moved. There! She felt it. The vibrations were tighter upstairs. With helping her aunt's friends, she learned early that the higher quality jewels always vibrated faster.

Her whole body resonated on the same level as the stone. She nearly laughed out loud. It was too easy. She was almost running along the corridor. Her feet trod silently on the plush carpet. At the third bedroom on the right she stopped abruptly and confidently opened the door. Standing at the center of the room, she pointed under the bed.

"Down there, under the bed."

The men were directly behind her and the closest nodded. Inclining his head at the others, they picked up the bed and shuffled it across the room. Placing it in the corner without a sound, they rolled the rug away from the polished wooden floor. Underneath Kiera saw a small hatch cut in the floorboards. As she watched, the first man opened a black doctor's bag he was carrying and carefully pried open the hatch with the tool he took from it.

Out of the way in the corner, she couldn't see clearly how he opened the safe. He listened hard while turning a dial and within moments, it was open. The man beckoned her to sit beside him.

Reluctantly she moved closer, kneeling by the open hatch. She looked at the man who nodded in response. She reached out and took out three velvet wrapped parcels from the hole laying them beside her. The man beside her reached out for them but she shook her head violently. Ignoring everything but the vibrations, she went straight to the bottom of the safe. She knew from the feel of the jewelry that the boxes beside her held only worthless costume fakes. The real diamonds were beneath.

Using her nails she scraped along the bottom. At the corner she located a small hole. Fitting her fingers through it she pulled. The bottom of the safe gave way to show another space beneath. Now the vibrations increased in intensity. They must have been encased in lead she thought. Grabbing a cream silk pouch she threw it at the men standing by her as if it burned her fingers.

"There they are!"

The tall man just laughed catching it.

"You won't be so dismissive when you get some of the profits from this baby!" But Kiera was ashamed, she had promised never to use her talent for anything illegal. She never told her aunt about the jewelry thefts - or any of her family. It was between her, her father and that horrible man.

On their way out, she saw a dying orchid beside the door. For some reason she felt compelled to touch the failing plant. For a second she felt dizzy as pure energy leapt from her finger. Confused, she stared at it. It seemed to be a little healthier than it had before. She shrugged her shoulders. She must have imagined it.

Since that time, she had met that man

countless times. She had learned to dread his approach, his gravelly voice. That first job appeared in the papers the following week. Her aunt read it aloud to her while her father was out. Kiera remembered that day clearly, when the paper reported that the orchid had miraculously recovered. The owners of the house thought it was strange the burglars would leave a healthy plant instead of their dead one. Her aunt had laughed at that. Why worry about a plant when they lost thousands of pounds in jewels?

Afterwards, Kiera had tried it again on some dying plants at the end of the camp. It took several tries but she found that she got stronger each time. Soon she was able to heal trees by a thought without even needing to touch them. From that point on every house she went to she made any plants she saw in the buildings healthy. The paper thought she replaced them but she knew better. It was the least she could do.

She hadn't done badly out of the arrangement. It wasn't as though any of those families were poor, Kiera reasoned as she tried to justify the memories to herself. They, no, she needed the money more. After each job, the man had given them some money. She would always hide away a third for herself. Her father wasn't around when the men brought the payment, so he never knew what it was. She was sure the man with the scar knew she kept some back but he never told her father if he did.

Dragging herself away from her memories, Kiera made her decision - it had to be now. It was time to go. She had just turned fifteen and she was heartily sick of the life. She had already put some of the money in an account and she knew where to go for a passport.

Her ability to read minds had come and gone often over the years, but it had given her some useful information. She knew how to pick locks, where to fence money and most important of all where to go for that all-important passport.

She knew the system but she also knew where to go next. Her aunt had told her of some family in the UK she could stay with. She needed to go to an English-speaking country she reasoned, and England would be the easiest to get to. If she stayed in Ireland her father would be able to find her eventually. The traveler community was not that large.

Stuffing the passport in with a spare set of clothes, she took one more look at the room. She wouldn't miss it - any of it. Not even her father. Her only remaining tie, her aunt, had died last year. She was finally free. Slinging the backpack over her shoulders, she made her way out to her new life.

Getting through customs concerned Kiera the most. She needn't have worried though; Campbell's mind had told her the name of the best forger in Ireland. Even so, passport control just waved her through. She didn't even have to open it!

As she strode through the station she contemplated her next move. She had to find her family. Taking a couple of hundred out of the cashpoint Kiera scanned the station for signs. The tube station was across the hall. Knowing the family was in Enfield she planned to take the Piccadilly line straight to Oakwood. Her cousins lived next to the park there.

She should have accepted Aunt Clara's offer. She had wanted to contact them before she died but Kiera had always refused. She didn't want to think about what would happen when Aunt Clara wasn't around anymore. If they didn't talk about it, it wouldn't happen. Life doesn't work that way she thought sadly. Standing on the platform, Kiera chewed her lip, pushing back the emotions. She missed her.

She knew the Jelleys would let her stay. Her aunt had told her how close she had been to her sister when she was younger.

Kiera took out her address book. She could read now. It had taken torturous months but her aunt had insisted on the lessons once she found about the thefts. Kiera had kept her vow to herself never to tell her aunt, but the wily older woman was wise enough to know that one day she would have to move on when she was old enough. To survive on her own, she would need to be able to read.

It had taken her a long time to get this far, finally to have independence. Kiera stepped on to the train and settled back in the seat.

The tube train soon filled up, and people of all types were packed in like sardines: business workers, tourists, housewives and shoppers. The acrid smell of so many people cramped in together was difficult to ignore. She wrinkled her nose but after a few minutes she got used to it. At each station more and more people joined the train. It was getting more and more difficult for people to get on and off.

Seated at the end of a row of seats nearest the door, Kiera had just enough space to ignore the discomfort of the other passengers. A woman, obviously pregnant, leant against the glass screen on her left. She had one hand holding on to the grips and her left-hand holding a paperback. As they reached Oxford Circus, the door began to open and close repeatedly. It jolted Kiera from her stupor. Realizing the discomfort the woman in front must be in, Kiera half-rose to give up her seat. Before she could, a tall man dressed in a scruffy creased pinstripe suit realized he was about to miss his stop. He began to elbow passengers out of his way with one arm and use his briefcase as a battering ram with the other. People began to shout as his briefcase hit thighs and elbows. He ignored them, desperate to get off.

The pregnant woman standing beside the door looked up but she didn't stand a chance. There was no room to get off and she didn't have time or the space to move out of his way. Kiera winced as he twisted and elbowed the woman in the stomach. The woman's gasp of pain resounded loudly in Kiera's mind. She felt as well as saw the woman collapse against the blue metal post.

Instinctively Kiera touched the woman. A flash of awareness greeted her - the baby was in trouble. She could feel the baby's heart miss a beat. The pendant under her shirt began to throb. Surprised she stared at the crystal at the end of its leather cord. That had never happened before. The distress of the baby once again called for her attention. Without knowing why, she placed her hand again over the woman's stomach. Using her new awareness and fleeting telepathy she reassured the fetus. At the same time, without knowing how, she erased the damage the man had done. As the woman hit the floor she knew the baby was all right. The mother would not even suffer a bruise.

Where the woman fell, a sudden vacuum was created. The man didn't even stop to see who he had hit but moved on shoving people out of his way, frantic not to miss his stop. As he ran on to the exit, the rest of the carriage emptied.

A student sitting on the opposite seat to Kiera saw the woman collapse on the floor. Rushing across to the expectant mother, the boy pulled her to her feet. Concerned, he stood in the doorway calling for a guard to get help. Sure the pregnant woman was being taken care of, Kiera leant back exhausted. Her whole body ached but she knew what she had just done was right. She had saved a life! She had not just imagined it, she had felt the tiny life and because of her, it was alive. The mother would never know, but she did. She smiled. Maybe she could atone for all she had done.

A few hundred miles away, Jake and Mirim faced each other on the corner by the school. Jake was staring at Mirim in disbelief.

Jake felt it first. Connected to the Matrix, Mirim experienced it only a few seconds later as it travelled through the psychic link.

"Did you feel that?" she breathed. She felt the tingle of raw power leave her senses.

"Yes." He said slowly.

"Someone used power! We need to find the other lost children of the Elementi. That had to be one!"

Jake squinted back at Mirim, "Lost children of the Elementi? That sounds like a bad sci-fi movie."

"A what? No, one of the Elementi. You are one, I am one. There are three others. I am from the family representing air; there is still earth, fire and water to find."

"What am I ?" He demanded.

"You, you are the spirit element. Your family's color is white. You represent the focus of all the powers. You can wield all four, but you do not have as much of any one power as we do individually. You are however more powerful for having all four. We need you to complete the Matrix. There are five points, four on the outside and one in the middle - you. Without you, the four elements can do a lot, but without you, neither Aras nor the Magi can be defeated."

As the Matrix transferred the coordinates of the energy surge, Mirim gazed into the distance, "I have the coordinates of where he or she was. From the data I downloaded from your networks, the power was most likely used on a train. I need you to concentrate on the power to find it. Now you know what it feels like you should be able to focus on it. Let the power draw you to it."

"How do I do that?"

Mirim held back her impatience. She had grown up with the Matrix so she knew how to use it. She had forgotten the younger boy was new to it.

"Listen, follow my thoughts." She hadn't done this since before her mother died. It was dangerous. You had to trust the other person implicitly. After this, he would know her better than she knew herself and vice versa.

Taking a deep breath, she reached out with her mind. Feeling her mind touch, Jake tentatively reached out with his. Memories flashed back and forth to each other at lightning speed. He caught her intense loneliness of being alone in the Citadel for years and the grief at her mother's death. How could she bear to be alone for that long? In his mind, she learned the thirst to find out about his parents, his heritage. She also saw the grief of losing his adopted parents and the wonder he felt at what was happening at that moment.

After the initial exchange, they turned to look at Jake's core of power. Visualizing it as a thin thread of power snaking through his body, she showed him how to match the power they had both felt against the four different colors making up the white cord. Tweaking each strand, they resonated at a different frequency. As Jake experimented on the green color, he knew he had it.

"That's the Earth element. She has an affinity with nature. She will be able to recognize metals or just make things grow better." Mirim explained.

She drew him along the yellow thread that kept her in contact with the Matrix mind back on Eleria. Fear gripped him as winds buffeted them in the no-space between worlds. He felt himself spin out of control, his mind was fragmenting and darkness began to encase Jake's mind. He was blown one way then another, there was no up or down, just endless night.

"Keep your mind focused on the yellow thread!" Mirim's voice admonished as if from a distance. Getting a hold of his mind, Mirim gathered him in her psychic embrace. Her skills were tested to her limit as his consciousness seemed to slither under her grasp. Finally stalling his spin, she sensed the Citadel near and dumped his mind through the conduits to the main crystal controls into the full mind meld. Now Mirim, Jake and the Matrix combined to make one vast but still incomplete mind.

"I couldn't do this on my own." He heard wonder in her thoughts. "I needed your abilities to do this." He knew how she felt - literally. He felt like he knew everything - could do anything.

He found his awareness spreading out though the planet of Eleria. Everywhere he looked there was crystal. He was the crystal. He understood how each crystal formed a part of the whole mind. "Wow, this is amazing." The Matrix couldn't think on its own. It used their minds. It was a partnership going back thousands of years.

He could sense it was grateful and even happy for him to be there. He felt an insane reciprocal happiness. It felt like home. The Matrix accepted him without any reservation. He now knew that Mirim, the Matrix and the others would be closer than any real family could ever be.

"Jake, you need to find that other element!" Her call brought him back to reality.

Leaving behind his own white cord so he could travel back if he needed to, he followed her by instinct. As his energy flowed into the Matrix, it multiplied. What he gave was given back to him threefold. Power called to like power and he felt himself moving at a great velocity back through the no-space to Earth. Still part of the whole, he found himself hovering above a girl. She could be no more than sixteen or seventeen at the most. She had long dark-brown hair. She was startlingly beautiful. She appeared to be sleeping on a train. As he watched, someone woke her up. This was the last stop on the line, the man told her. She twisted to look through the window at the sign for confirmation and nodded sleepily. After thanking the man, she left the train. Jake made a note of the name, Oakwood.

Mirim instructed the Matrix to disconnect their minds and to send them bodily to Oakwood. If they hurried, they would hopefully be able to catch her before she went any further.

CHAPTER SEVEN
- SHENELLA

Shenella squinted into the far corner of the Great Hall. Marta and Ecu were leaning towards each other by the buffet table, obviously talking in whispers even though no one would be able to hear them in the general din even had they been talking normally. *What could they be talking about? Really, if you are going to plot something, don't act as if you are! They are spending far too much time together,* she thought. *What are they doing?*

She was shocked at how quickly Ecu was rising at court. It seemed everywhere she turned he was there with that sly grin. And the way the First Adviser was dismissed - no good could come of it. She could already see Aras' other advisers getting restless. He was talking to them less and less each day. That could only cause trouble.

The advisers were powerful people in their own right. If he continued to ignore them, it would betray his weakness. It was only a matter of time before someone took his or her chance.

She could understand that Aras would favor Ecu a little. After all, he had lessened his headaches when no one else could, but this was ridiculous. How could a simple healer rise so high? *Of course,* she answered herself, *he was no simple healer!* He was also a magician as well as a scholar, all that drivel about his 'research in the Great Library' on his first day. The Council had been advisers to the throne for decades. One adviser she believed had even served under the first Aras - her fiancé's grandfather.

From her vantage point in the corner, Shenella had an uninhibited view of the entire room. No one paid any attention to her sitting by the doorway. It was as if she didn't exist to them. If they thought about her at all, it was probably like the throne that Aras sat on each and every day she mused. There, important because he needed something to sit on but in itself not worth thinking about. Part of her of course was grateful. She wasn't stupid. People disappeared or died regularly in the court for being noticed. She had no discernible power as the Magi recognized it, so she was not considered a threat. There were benefits to being invisible but it did irk her sometimes!

Ecu moved away from Marta and began to work his way around the different factions in the room. She began to notice it yesterday. First, he spoke to the head of the merchants' union, the lowlanders. The islanders were next and now he was talking to the Ambassador to the Merpeople.

Although it was not recognized or even visible by the Magi she did have some of the old power. *And now*, she thought, *this was the time to use it.* Shenella sidled up to the table nearest Ecu. The combination of her status as being the future consort to the Emperor and her power to stop people noticing her was a potent one. She imagined a shield protecting her from people's minds. *Either one makes me invisible*, she thought with a wry smile. *Maybe next year when we are actually married I will be someone.* She shivered at the thought. *Yes, but at what price?*

She was close enough now to study the Ambassador's features. She had never seen this man before. One of the servants had told her earlier this was his first time in Naven. He looked just like anyone else in the room but Shenella knew better. The only visible difference to the casual observer was his hair. It had a strange greeny-blue tinge to it. His face was ordinary, grey eyes, aquiline nose and a balanced jaw.

The way he held himself though showed her he was younger than most of the other ambassadors. He seemed confident but there was an undertone of nervousness about him. In his twenties she guessed. Merpeople were rarely seen outside their own domain. They coexisted peacefully with the islanders, spending most of their time in their underwater cities before having to go back to land.

All the other Ambassadors were probably in their second to third life cycle. One of the perks of being or helping the Magi was mind transference to another's body when the original reached old age. It was the reason they were all so good-looking she supposed. There was no reason why they would choose ugly people to take over.

I wonder what happens to the people they were, she wondered. *Are they still in there? Or was their consciousness pushed out to be eaten by the Gods?* She shivered. At least she would never suffer that fate. Without warning the Ambassador looked her way. He stared straight into her eyes and gave her a small smile. He winked.

Startled, she averted her eyes. He could *see* her. Mechanically she picked up a sweet cake from one of the silver platters beside her. One of the first warnings she had heard when she arrived a few years before had been that it was unwise to eat the food laid out in the Great Hall. The funny thing was they all thought it was poisoned. Stupid, each person thought that one of the others had poisoned the food so no one bothered to do it. Besides she had seen one of the castle's tame crows eating one of the cakes earlier and it would have been dead by now if it was tainted. She took a bite. *Ugh, it tasted like sawdust.* The cooks obviously didn't bother to make their sweets tasty for the same reason.

She tuned back into their conversation.

"Sori, you have to understand. The Elementi are nearly all dead. Soon the entire civilized world will be under the control of the two Magi Empires. Why not pledge your allegiance fully now? The Merpeople won't stand a chance against the Empire's military and once the last of the Elementi has been eliminated, well, Aras will turn to the independent states. Even underwater you will not be safe. And we all know that you can't stay under there forever."

"Surely not," the Ambassador replied, "I have assurances from Aras himself that he will let my people be as long as we give him his yearly tribute."

"Yes, but why settle for a yearly tribute when the Empire can have everything?"

"You know this for certain?"

"Of course no one can tell the Emperor's mind but I have it on good authority that Aras' policies will change soon."

With the Ambassador in confusion Ecu left to talk to the Chirrian representative nearby. Sori lost in thought, went to re-join his party. Shenella was about to follow Ecu when the speaker at the door announced that Aras was now ready for petitions. All in the room craned their necks to watch for his entrance.

Ecu disappeared as the room melted to the sides to make way for Aras. All thoughts of him ended when she saw Aras' figure enter. To Shenella's eyes, Aras looked every inch the arrogant Emperor. His dark blonde hair was slicked back from his face. His mouth was pursed in a straight line, his head held high. How she hated him!

To begin with she didn't want anything to do with Aras and his infernal court. Her parents had been supportive. They were frightened of him, but at the same time they were one of the oldest families in Eleria. Her family had a proud history. They had been friends and advisers to countless Elementi rulers in the past. They thought their status would protect them as it had since the Change.

Shenella recalled her governess's words. After the coup, Rayse Deveaux, the great-grandmother of the current Emperor had formed a government that took over the old Elementi Empire - lock, stock and barrel. "Why bother to make your own Empire when there was one already made?" the governess had asked. But where the Elementi ruled by trade and politics, the Magi used force, fear and illusion.

Successive governments had managed to keep the structure together with a harsh hand but Aras had changed over the last few years. She had watched him reach out to the breakaway and independent states since she had been in court, hence the daily audiences. No one knew why he changed, but Shenella had heard a rumor that his mother made him promise before she died. He in turn had to wait until he was crowned before he could change anything.

Shenella could not help it but each time she saw him she was reminded of her parent's death. She was told it was an accident - that her parents had left the city a day early, that halfway home a stray stone in the road had jarred the carriage. The horses in their panic had jerked forward. The couplings had snapped and the carriage had careered off the cliff to the beach below.

Each time she remembered, it was as if she relived the memories. A few days after it had happened, her family's stern lawyer, his face craggy and sorrowful, had sat her down in the gloom of his over-furnished office. Her parents had been his friends for many years as well as just clients. As she stared at the old leather-bound volumes behind him, he explained how the coachman was thrown clear before the coach left the cliff. The coachman had raced down to the beach but it was too late - her parents were dead.

"Where was Yeru?" she had asked him. She had not seen the gruff coachman since he left with her parents. It would never have happened if he had been driving. Patiently, the lawyer explained that he was taken ill suddenly the night before and they had hired a coachman from the local stables. His relatives in the city were looking after him and there would be no point coming back until the estate was settled.

She knew at that moment it was no accident. The accident must have been deliberate. It was too much of a coincidence. Within days of her parents' death, the court had appointed new guardians. They were good people the lawyer tried to reassure her. They were also from an established family, high at court. Shenella shivered, if she knew what she knew now - she would have tried to run away.

She had to go immediately, the lawyer told her, and his tone turned apologetic. He walked to the door and ushered in a stern looking woman who had been sitting quietly in the outer office.

"This is Vel. She has been hired to escort you to your new home." Vel stood up and nodded. Shenella recognized from her dress that she must be one of the nomadic people who hired themselves out as escorts and fighters. Nervously, Shenella's fingers played with the satin purse strings on her lap.

"It's all right, Shenella, she'll make sure you arrive safely."

She was given no time to pack, but there was plenty of time to think on the journey. From the lawyer's office, Vel took her straight to the coach. She was only allowed to bring what she had with her at the time, a small travelling bag and her small dog, Friel.

Three days of hard travel later with stops only to change the horses and refreshments, she arrived at what she believed was to be her new home. Although Vel hadn't said a word since they met, she still felt abandoned when the older lady left. As soon as her feet touched the gravel, she knew there was no going back. Her parents were never coming back.

Still in shock, she was met by Lord Reik himself. He stood waiting alone, impatiently stamping his feet on the decorative gravel to keep warm outside his grand home. He wore dark clothes and from his immaculate suit to his highly polished boots. Shenella knew that this was a man to be wary of.

The house was an imposing building surrounded by well-kept formal gardens. Given the obvious wealth of her new guardians she was surprised to find no household line-up to greet her. However, with no one around, he made no bones about her new position. He was in charge and she was going to marry the

Emperor-King when she came of age - whether she liked it or not.

Lord and Lady Reik had tried to convince her with words at first.

"You'll get the best dresses, Shenella, as well as the finest food." She could still hear *that* woman's voice in her head. No matter how they painted the life as glamorous, she knew the truth. Life as a consort to an Arellian monarch was a fate worse than death. She still refused so they took Friel away... as well as the few keepsakes she had with her.

Years before, in her parent's library, she had read stories of past consorts, silly women she had thought with scorn. They were like dolls, no will of their own and only there to look good on the Emperor's arm and of course to provide the next generation. They were beautiful - she conceded that. The pictures on the walls of Aras' apartment she saw later proved it. She had to admit that was flattering. Some of those past queens however did not always live a long life. They certainly never outlived the Emperor they married.

It had only taken her new guardians two weeks to break her - to send the message to the Council of her consent. She endured two long weeks of beatings and deprivation. She wanted to be stronger, like the heroines in the books she read from before the Arellian Empire - but at the thought of the pain, her eyes clouded. They had only given her enough food and water to keep her alive.

Even so she could have resisted. Lord Reik forbade all her old friends from seeing her. Cut off from her old life they locked her in an empty room. The first night they locked her up she had made a pillow of her coat to sleep on the dirty wooden floor. They waited just until her breathing evened and woke her up. Every time she was near sleep a servant was told to go in to wake her up again - and they did.

It wasn't long before she was near breaking point. A mere ten days after her arrival, her health was failing. Fearing repercussions if they failed, the Reiks did the last and worst thing they could think to do.

The door opened quietly enough the night she capitulated. Lord Reik walked in carrying Friel. Weak as she was, she managed a small smile. He dropped the puppy on the floor and it ran to her, happy to see his mistress again. She honestly thought they had reconsidered - that they had a change of heart. Reaching out she half sat up and lifted Friel into her lap. Her mood lifted as she stroked the soft golden fur.

Friel was a gift from her parents a few months before their death. Now she was the only reminder of a happier time. The puppy too was ecstatic at being reunited with his mistress. He licked her face and squirmed joyfully on her lap. Shenella was speechless with gratitude.

"Will you marry Lord Aras?" Lord Reik intoned kneeling beside her.

"What? ...I don't understand" Shenella mumbled confused. The puppy snuggled closer, yapping quietly.

"I'll ask again, will you marry Lord Aras?"

"No!"

The man stood, his face set hard as granite only inches from her face.

"You leave me no choice." Reaching into his pocket, he brought out a small hunting knife. He held it up for her to have a good look. The light from the high window glinted on its shiny surface. Shenella's eyes swiveled fearfully from the knife to his face and back, pulling the puppy tight against her.

"N-no, you wouldn't." Her eyes pleaded with his.

He ignored her and grabbed the small animal from her roughly. His manservant, who she hadn't noticed come in, stood nearby.

"Hold her!" Lord Reik ordered.

With an apologetic shrug the man gripped her. She struggled to look away but his hold was strong. Every time she moved her head, he twisted her so she faced Lord Reik. She watched with growing horror as Lord Reik plunged the knife into the heart of the frightened puppy. Friel jerked and gave one last small yelp of pain and fear and died.

She didn't want to believe it had happened, but her mind couldn't deny the evidence. There was silence for a moment - pierced by her scream. She couldn't stop. The manservant let her go. Reik tried to say something but the grief was too much. She'd lost her parents and now her last companion. She was alone. All the grief she had been holding back took over. They left her alone with the small dead dog as a reminder.

The next day she agreed to the marriage.

Watching him dealing with petitioners on the throne, Shenella considered what she had learnt since. In the last couple of years she had grown to know Aras, although he wasn't as bad as she first thought, she still hated him for taking away her life. She blamed him almost as much as she blamed herself for her parents' death.

She felt conflicted. Of course he was cruel - but not to her. She understood him better now, even though she didn't agree with his methods. One person could change history. Hadn't his great, great-grandmother brought down the powerful Elementi Empire? Maybe she could change Aras? She hated him but as her parents would say, two wrongs did not make a right.

In the corner, Marta was defending herself to Ecu.

"I just haven't been able to get close to him. He is never on his own. A couple of days ago he holed up in the anteroom for some reason. He didn't come out until this morning and he called a meeting of the generals. He'd think it was strange if I turned up to that!"

"Well, you'll just have to find a way to do it tonight. I've done my part, I've talked to all the people we need to get on our side first and got the others thinking. We need to control Aras, and soon." Marta nodded in silent agreement.

CHAPTER EIGHT
- SPELLED

It had been a long day, Aras thought as he stretched his muscles. He raised his arms over his head, letting the muscles tighten then loosen. Things were a lot easier in father's time. Merchants want to pay less tax? Send the militia in. Farmers providing less grain? Send the militia in. In fact any problems just send the militia in. He grimaced. Diplomacy was so wearing. He had a good mind to just go with the Council and follow his father's example... but the savings in military costs outweighed any gains made by force. Again, it would be a lot easier just to leave it to the generals.

He thought again about the meeting this morning. The mercenaries still hadn't found anything about the Citadel. Adramelech hadn't reported about the boy either. He'd give him another day he decided. Aras stood up and began to pace the room, studiously ignoring the maid tidying across from him. He could feel the glimmerings of a headache beginning to throb in his temple.

"Marta." He called out into the corridor. Marta hastened into the room. She curtsied and bowed her head.

"Yes, my lord?"

"Get me a drink and one of those pills Ecu made."

"Yes, my Lord." This was it. She grinned. Hiding her smile, she turned away. Marta stepped over to the window first and pulled the heavy wooden shutters across the glass. In the resultant gloom, she quietly ushered out the maid who had been making the bed. Following the maid out, she stooped to light a candle outside the room.

Back inside, she opened a small gilt cabinet beside the bed and took out the small box of pills Ecu had given Aras. She reached up to pick up the water jug and poured half a glass. Darting a glance behind her, she prayed the powder would be tasteless as well as colorless. She held out her left-hand over the glass and lightly pressed the sides of the ring. The ruby popped up, releasing the white powder into the glass. Swirling the mixture, she turned gracefully to hand the drink and pill to Aras.

"Here, my Lord."

"Thanks." His voice was terse although grateful enough.

The headache was intense now, the throbbing behind the eyes like an axe hitting the walls in a Salarian mine. Aras closed his eyes to control the pain. He cradled the glass for a moment and took a deep swig of water. Placing the tablet on his tongue, he jerked his head back to swallow the mixture. His head tingled pleasantly. It hadn't done that before; maybe Ecu had improved the recipe?

Marta positioned herself in front of him. As she did so, the door to the side opened unexpectedly. Aras faced the door, his eyes flying open in anger. Everyone knew to leave him alone when the candle was lit!

At that, he saw her. H actually saw her. It was if she suddenly popped into existence before him. The pain in his head receded to be replaced by another pain deep in his heart. He knew she hadn't wanted to come to the castle. He hadn't murdered her parents personally but he knew for a fact he was the reason they died. He remembered the flippant remark to his first adviser as if it were yesterday.

"I don't care how you do it, but make sure she will be my wife."

He hadn't given it a moment's thought before now. The pain twisted like a knife in his heart at the realization.

Shenella stood in the doorway confused. Marta was here? Aras and Marta stood in front of her. Aras looked strange... in pain. Shenella swiveled to look at the other occupant, Marta... If looks could kill, Shenella thought wryly, I would be ash on the floor right now.

She didn't know what had just happened but Shenella knew something was up. She'd seen the candle and thought that perhaps now would be a good time to talk to Aras. If she could foil a plot maybe he would trust her. From there... who knows? She hadn't thought any further than that. Seeing Marta there, she retreated. She wasn't silly enough to say anything with her there.

Aras stepped towards her, his palms upturned.

"Shenella, my love, don't go." He put both arms out and touched her fingertips. He drew her to him. Not even acknowledging Marta, he dismissed her.

Furious Marta stared disbelievingly as the

couple embraced. Her mouth opened and closed with a snap. This was ridiculous. She stalked to the door. She had to find Ecu quickly. Hopefully the potion was reversible. Racing through corridors reserved for servants, she pushed through, leaving startled glances in her wake. She reached Ecu's rooms out of breath. She paused before the door to compose herself. Brushing her dark hair back, she took a moment before opening the door calling his name. She found him in what used to be the servant rooms of the suite.

He had been busy in the last few days, she thought, noting the changes. He had managed to get the castle carpenters to convert the existing furniture into a laboratory in record time. Where once there stood bunk beds, dressers and cupboards, now tables covered every inch of available space. Every surface was covered with jars, test tubes, burners and such occult equipment she had no hope of ever understanding.

"It didn't work," she said as she burst into the room.

"What didn't work?" He calmly poured two colorless liquids together.

"The powder, the love potion - it didn't work!"

He set the mixture down, "Calm down. It was

only supposed to last a couple of hours anyway. I thought that something like this would happen. ...By the way, what did happen?"

"That stupid creature-in-waiting got in the way. It was going perfectly. He asked me to prepare him a drink with one of those tablets you made him. I managed to get the powder in the glass without him suspecting. Just as he took the draught, that ninny walked in.

"Ah, right. I made that potion to last only a couple of hours for just such an event. If it had been successful we could have topped it up with ease at our leisure... and if you failed it wouldn't do too much damage. You'll have to try again later. He won't remember." Ecu waved his hand to dismiss her.

"It would have worked this time, if it wasn't for that interfering idiot!"

The healer peered over the jar he was holding.

"I told you it's all right." His voice was reassuring. "The precognition told me something like this could happen. You can sometimes change fate but in this case, obviously not. I knew something would go wrong, I just didn't know what."

"If you can tell the future, why couldn't you just tell me it wouldn't work that way and I would have done it differently?"

Ecu placed the jar he had been holding carefully on the nearest clear surface. He didn't have time for this. Patiently he explained, "I can see into other dimensions. Do you know what they are?" She shook her head. He continued as if to a young child.

"There are other worlds, almost exactly like this one. Each dimension is another world. There are an infinite number of them and each is subtly or not so subtly different."

Marta's face looked blank. With a sigh, Ecu explained further. "You can use the other dimensions to find out what will happen in the future. What makes each world different is that something happened which could have two outcomes. The worlds split apart at that difference. In some of those dimensions things worked a little quicker than others so some of them are in the past and some of them are in the future. I look for our neighboring dimensions, which are closest to ours but set a little in the future. I saw several things go wrong. In some you were successful, in others Shenella walks in, or another maid. Aras sees you putting the potion into the glass in still others. I couldn't possibly tell you which one it would be. I can just work to certain possibilities."

"What use is this power if there are so many possibilities that you can't find out what the future will hold?"

"Trends, my dear girl. I know roughly what will happen because it appears in so many realities. I knew, for instance, that our partnership would be the one most likely to lead to success."

"All right, how long will the potion last?" Marta was only slightly mollified.

"Two hours, and you can try again. He won't remember. The subject who he saw – Shenella, wasn't it? - She will be a bit confused, but she won't know what changed him. Here." He pulled a small box from his robe. "Fill your ring up, you'll have to try again."

Sighing, Marta took the box and left the room.

CHAPTER NINE
- ADRAMELECH

"I just don't understand why I can't sense the others' powers." Jake was out of breath. They'd materialized at Oakwood station moments earlier and immediately started running to the exit.

"They have to use them first. It's a self-defense mechanism," Mirim explained. "They can't use their magic properly until you use yours first. You are what they called in the old days a catalyst. You can't sense them until theirs has activated. And they can't activate fully until you have used your powers at least once. It happens in each generation"

She raised her hand to shield her eyes from the bright sun. "Can you see her yet?"

They were walking past the taxi rank through

the car park. Oakwood Park lay across the road from them. Beyond the fence the green and yellow fields were separated neatly by hedges, creating an untidy patchwork effect. The countryside view in front of them was a stark contrast to the industrialized town behind them.

Checking she hadn't gone south along the other road, Jake moved to the edge of the parking area. It was past rush hour and he could clearly see that none of the few people there were the almond-eyed girl he saw on the train. Next, he checked along the row of buildings to the left of the station. The glass shop fronts revealed these were also empty.

"We must have missed her!" He said frustrated. "I can hardly feel her now."

Mirim thoughtfully gazed into the fields. "The park is protecting her."

"What?"

"Sorry I forgot to mention that if one of us is near a concentrated source of our element, we are practically invisible next to it. That park must be miles long. The combined effect of all that wildlife would interfere with her resonance. We'll have to wait until she goes into the city or uses her power again."

Suddenly the whole situation was too much

for Jake.

"This is completely ridiculous! I have a life! I shouldn't be traipsing around looking for God knows who, who can do God knows what."

Mirim dropped her hands to her sides and looked at Jake in dismay. "Jake you are the next High-King, we need you. Without you we cannot possibly defeat the Magi - or even reunite the Elementi again."

"It's not my problem is it? That's another world. I live in this one. What do I care if some mad magician wants to take over your world? It's not as if he can come to this one is it?"

"Well, yes he can. Of course he can. He may not be able to travel inter-dimensionally as we can but he could easily get someone who can. He must know you are active by now; you both have the same power. Every time you used your crystal it will have affected him in some way. Don't ask me how," she forestalled. "There are creatures that can traverse the dimensions as easily as we breathe. All he has to do is compel one to bring him here. With his Magi side he should be able to do that easily enough. I'm surprised he hasn't done this already to be honest. It would be dangerous, but possible."

"Well he hasn't. If I don't bother him, maybe

he won't bother me." About to use the Matrix to go home, he paused. How quickly it had become a part of him he realized. He glowered at Mirim. He couldn't use the crystal, it might alert the Emperor. With a deep sigh, he went back to the tube station. It would take several hours to get back the old-fashioned way.

"Jake! Wait! It will only be a matter of time before Aras sends someone to kill you. He has to. If he doesn't, he will die. The more your power grows the more the Elementi power gets stronger and it will make him weaker."

"By that reasoning, if I don't use my power, it won't get stronger." He continued to walk away.

"It's too late, once you started using your powers they won't go away," she called. "It will just increase until you learn control."

"Whatever!"

Furious Mirim paced up and down the pavement. Stupid boy, he wasn't safe. No one was safe. She wasn't going to let their parents' sacrifices go to waste!

She sent her mind back to the Matrix. The girl had used her 'magic' for want of a better word. There just had to be a way to trace her. The girl's element was a direct complement or opposite of her own. There had to be a way she could find her without Jake. Jake would come around, he just needed some time to himself.

Spotting a handy brick wall Mirim sat down to wait. The girl would use her power soon - she wouldn't be able to help it. When she did, Mirim would be waiting.

Adramelech materialized in real-space. On all four sides were white painted buildings with a small park in the center. He stood in the doorway of a shop with a Corinthian pillar obscuring him from passers-by. The tinkling of the tall fountain to his right assaulted his senses after the quiet of no-space. People were milling in twos and threes quietly chatting as they went in and out of shops.

Quickly cloaking himself in skin and robe, Adramelech stopped to observe a man passing. Noting the style, he copied his clothes. His long black robe morphed to form blue jeans and a short, red jacket. Checking his reflection in the shop window Adramelech compared himself with other shoppers. Standard fare he thought. There doesn't seem to be any originality in this place. He grimaced. Humans. He just didn't understand why some of the brethren liked them.

He shook his head. To him they were a means

to end. With the power of the Citadel he could return to his own world and get revenge on those that had banished him. He'd searched countless dimensions for something, which would help. It was by pure luck that Aras had called him and not one of the others. That was the ignorance of the Magi. They could call his people. They could command them but they didn't understand what they held. They were too blinded by greed to bother to find out.

Adramelech snarled. His people, who they called demons, were exiles. After his banishment from Earth, his people had labeled him a criminal and a troublemaker. They didn't have prisons as other worlds knew them so they banished people like him to the no-space between dimensions. Without bearings you could be right beside a reality and not know it. Trapped there, he'd been fully aware but without a way to form a body. This was far more effective for his kind than any prison could ever be.

The sun was high in the sky - midday he thought. Time worked differently between the worlds. It could take an instant, hours, days or even years to travel the vast distances among them. He could have been floating in no-space for thousands of years before Aras had called him. Travel between the dimensions was an imprecise science among his people. Once the knowledge to cross the dimensions with accuracy was basic knowledge to even the simplest Deoc, but that knowledge was lost before his lifetime.

He sniffed the air. There was something about this place. He felt as if he'd been here before. He'd been to a great many worlds but this one had a familiar feel... It would come back to him, but he'd better recharge first. Fighting Aras' control had sapped more strength than he had first thought. He needed some power and he needed it soon.

Starving, he stretched his awareness. Great place to land he thought - no volcanoes for hundreds of miles. Spreading himself thinly he let his core substance float upwards. He let it flow where it needed to go.

His body disintegrated into steam as he rose higher into the atmosphere. The higher he got the further his awareness was able to cover, seeking the intense heat of an active volcano. Suddenly he saw it. Passing the body of water, he crossed land. Drawing nearer he started to recognize it. "I have been here before - of all the luck!"

Circling the islands off the land mass he

found several viable volcanoes. For nostalgia's sake he glided down to a volcano he had used before. Adramelech coalesced back into his human form behind a lone tourist. This was the place. Of course it had been more active in the past. This volcano hadn't erupted for at least a hundred years. Never mind it wouldn't take too much to find what he needed - even if it was dormant now.

He was only here to feed he reminded himself. The compulsion to complete his task was strong. Damn the Magi and their powers. He would only be able to delay for a few minutes.

The people here he remembered were primitive. He laughed at his first memory of this place. He recalled how some natives had stood transfixed as they saw him transform from flames to look like them. *Superstitious idiots,* he had thought.

The Elder of the tribe had followed him to the mouth of the volcano. Ignoring him - the man was no threat to him - Adramelech walked into the red-hot lava, letting himself melt slowly, luxuriating in the creep of energy as it surrounded him.

With no compulsion, he had spent days in there. For brief bursts he could take energy from ordinary fire but a volcano was by far the best form of energy. When he re-emerged, he was curious to find the Elder was still there. He must have left and returned though because behind the little man stood a crowd of his friends.

In the days he had been gone they had built a crude camp. The tents were made with fur, surrounding a long campfire. The Elder who had originally followed him indicated for him to follow him to the fireside. Adramelech followed, bemused.

At the fire were what must have been the rest of the man's tribe. It was a ragtag crowd of around thirty, he guessed. There were more men than women, all dressed in furs. To the rear of the group, a woman stood slightly apart. Her red-rimmed eyes showed she'd been crying heavily. Crooning to a child in her arms, she tried to ignore the signals from the Elder for her to join them.

One of the men moved to grab hold of the baby. The woman resisted, holding it tighter. Another man parted from the crowd and struck her while the first grabbed the child. It began to cry. They placed the baby on the mud floor in front of the Elder. It looked up and began to move away to the right, the light and the crackling of the fire attracting it. The Elder smiled and grabbed it. Picking it up he offered it to Adramelech with a nod.

Adramelech shook his head, not understanding what the man wanted, Adramelech looked from the man to the baby and sneered in contempt. What would he do with a human child?

The Elder's smile faded, the God didn't understand. He pointed to Adramelech, the child and the fire. Finally realizing that the fiery spirit was not interested in taking the baby, the Elder threw the baby at the fire. The mother screamed and ran to the edge. The men who took the baby grabbed her arms as she passed them to hold her back. She struggled, but they were too strong. She shrieked incoherently - desperate to get to her child. They held her for a few moments more before allowing her to run to the fire. Mercifully the baby died instantly, its small head crushed by a sharp branch.

These people had to be the most primitive Adramelech had ever seen.

...but he began to see the possibilities.

Those people were a pathetic malnourished group of nomads when he found them but by the time he left, they were a force to be reckoned with. Under his guidance, the camp evolved into a huge city split into two, controlling most of the continent. He reveled in the memories. The power he had wielded. He could destroy whole armies just by pointing at them with fire. The dying screams were music to his ears. Battle after battle his people fought and won. The indigenous people no match for his power. He reveled in the adulation.

That was until news reached the Atlanteans. They were a clever people. They'd hidden their city under water so he hadn't known of their existence until it was too late. They'd captured him surprisingly easily. The Atlanteans knew there was nothing on Earth that could hold him for long, so they had summarily banished him. One minute he was at the head of an army, weapon in hand, rallying his men. Their answering shouts instilling glorious fear in the enemy. The next, nothingness, he was between worlds. Of course he tried to get back. Earth had easy pickings for a creature like him, but they sent him too far away - he couldn't get his bearings.

Luckily, or not so luckily as it turned out, he had managed to get home. When his people found out what he had done, they banished him as well, but this time it was done properly.

Adramelech mentally thanked Aras. If he couldn't defeat the boy-king, which was frankly ludicrous, he would find a way to break the compulsion and just take over this world. They may not be as primitive as when he was last here but they hadn't met anything like him for a thousand years.

His thoughts returning to the present day, Adramelech stood surveying the edge of the crater. Sulfuric steam belched from underground - a perfect way in.

The tourist finishing his photo of the village moved his camera around the rim of the crater. He wanted to get a panoramic of the sea next. The tripod juddered as it scraped against volcanic rock. The picture blurred as he focused the lens. Tapping it he saw Adramelech through the viewfinder. He blinked. He hadn't been there moments before. He blinked again. The man was melting?

As he watched, Adramelech let his true form burn the veneer he'd created. Giving a wave to the nonplussed visitor, he jumped into the vent.

Oh, he'd missed this. He plunged deep into the core. The heat was glorious. One little push here and the whole volcano would spurt into the sky devouring the whole island. The raw energy seeped into his being. As he grew stronger his awareness exulted in the feeling of power. He twisted and turned through the tunnels created by the latent steams of lava, it was just too tempting. Besides, that man had seen far too much.

Floating towards the nearest tectonic plate he began to push. Cracks began to appear and the hot magma bubbled. He pushed harder. Suddenly there was a resounding crack and the crust covering the top collapsed. With a rush, the red fiery mixture of molten gas and rocks, kept in for hundreds of years, leapt into the air to form a black cloud of ash high above the island of Vulcano.

Fully charged and aware the volcano could not hurt him, Adramelech melted into steam. He rode the current into the cloud and floated above it. The cloud was expanding rapidly; it was beginning to collapse under its own weight. To Adramelech's amusement he saw the tourist running down the volcanic face. The man was overweight and gasping for breath. There was no way he would be able to outrun the flow of fire and lava.

Hot red stones fell, forcing the man to

change his course continually. Thick lava spilled over the edge of the crater, pouring faster and faster as the extra weight pushed it along. The man craned his neck and saw it gathering speed. Panicked, he tried to run faster but tripped over an abandoned drinks-can. He fell heavily to his knees. He just had time to scream once before the lava overtook him - erasing all trace of his body.

Floating above the cloud, Adramelech felt the compulsion tighten around his consciousness. He remembered why he was here - the boy. He had to find that boy. Reaching out with his awareness, he searched for the recent use of the spirit element. There was none but a small trace to the west suggested there had been a few days ago. Recalling one of the forms he had chosen in the past, the Deoc compacted his energies, drawing them in to a tight kernel of power deep within him. There was a large clap of thunder and he transmuted mid-air into a gold and red-feathered bird. Comfortable in the familiar phoenix form, he unfurled his new wings and flew to investigate.

CHAPTER TEN
- EARTH QUEEN

Kiera leant against the hard metal of the bus stop. The number 377 had just passed without stopping and the timetable said there wouldn't be another for 20 minutes. As she waited she began to feel a strange pressure building beneath her. Her head jerked up and she looked around at the other people waiting but everyone else had the same bored expression they held moments before. No one else seemed to be noticing anything different.

An energy surge made her blink and the crystal under her shirt began to glow an iridescent green. At the same time she began to feel the pressure underneath her intensify. It was as if the Earth itself was under stress. Her body hummed in response. She took out her crystal and cupped it in her left hand. Tiny pinpoints of light danced in its depths and she became mesmerized by its beauty. The crystal almost seemed to be telling her something. It was tantalizing, almost beyond her reach, then she understood. Compelled to answer the call of distress - she now instinctively knew what to do.

Directing her mind down through the pavement, she felt the slow mind of the Earth's crust. It was slow, alien and... in pain she decided. She pictured the Earth deep underneath, trying to follow the source of the pain. Her geography was hazy but she knew as she travelled west, that her mind had left the UK, passed France and on into Italy.

Arriving at the source, she was horrified at the chaos she saw. Somehow the plates were pushed further away than they should be. She could feel the Earth's pain as if it were her own. Her arms ached as if stretched beyond their limits, held fast in a medieval torture device. Her mind raced and she realized she needed to make it cooler first. Kiera drew the heat away into the nearby sea, simultaneously assessing the damage.

It felt wrong, the plates needed to be closer to heal the rift. *How had they moved so far apart?* She concentrated, aligning herself to the tectonic plates. They felt as if they were part of her. Kiera pictured the plates fully in her mind as extensions to her arms, she began to pull them slowly together. It was slow and they felt so heavy. As her hands drew together, in reality the plates grew closer, until finally judging by feel they were where they should have been only minutes before.

Back in London, Mirim also knew exactly when the Earthquake hit. The work Kiera was doing was too late for the village at the bottom of the volcano. As the lava encased the houses, a thousand minds went silent. The chatter of their minds had been a drop in the ocean a few moments ago but their sudden absence was more profound to Mirim than anything she had experienced before.

Mirim raised her head, tears streaming down her cheeks. So many dead! Her eyes focused at the bus stop across the road. While she had been standing with Jake, the street lamp opposite them had blocked their view, but now, sat on the low brick wall she could see her. The girl from the train was sitting directly across from her.

Mirim rose to her feet, she had to get to her before a bus did. She raced to the pedestrian crossing only meters away. As she ran, a double-decker red bus paused to let her cross. Seeing the girl rise to her feet at the bus stop, she knew she must not let her get on that bus.

She wished Jake were there; he could have easily melted the engine. Or if she had been a water power, she could have flooded it. This was no computerized car such as they had at the Citadel. She had to influence the driver. Her mother's words came back to her. You must never use your power to control others. Mirim knew it was unethical. Her mother had made her promise on the family's honor to never to use her power to overshadow or control others against their will.

Standing in the middle of the pedestrian crossing she faced a dilemma. If she let the girl get on the bus, it might be hours or days before she could trace her again. It might be too late. She knew she had to do it now when it was safe to do so. She sent waves of thought to the driver and passengers. *'The bus has broken down,'* she transmitted. She repeated the message again and again. *'The bus has broken down; we might as well get off. The bus has broken down, we may as well get off.'*

Mechanically the driver pulled the handbrake and shouted instructions to the passengers.

"Everybody off! The next bus will be along shortly."

As if sleepwalking, the driver and passengers filed off leaving the bus parked in front of the crossing.

Relieved, Mirim rushed to the bus stop to talk to the girl. As she approached, the girl was looking at her oddly. Mirim pulled the other girl's name from her mind.

"Kiera, my name is Mirim Ariel. I really need to talk with you."

"Who are you? How do you know my name?"

"Mirim. This is not the place. Something big has just happened and from the look of you, you know what it was. Let's go into the park."

Confused, Kiera just stared back at the blond girl. There was no way she was going with this stranger. Exasperated, Mirim slipped into the girl's thoughts. She didn't have time for this! In a split-second she told Kiera about Eleria, the Citadel, who she was, what she was and what she was about to do.

Knowing the other girl would not be as experienced as her, she watched Kiera's eyes widen as she clamped her own awareness around the girl's mind. Mirim knew it was wrong but this was urgent, she had to do it. Their whole world was at stake. She commanded the earth talent to follow her. The girl's mind fluttered in response, seeking to escape its cage but she was no match for Mirim. With expert skill she cut off every escape route mercilessly until her mind was still.

As if in a daze, Kiera nodded. She picked up her rucksack, balanced against the signpost and trailed behind her weaving through the abandoned passengers. She was petrified. She couldn't escape the grasp of the alien mind surrounding her. Today she'd escaped her life in Ireland, saved a baby's life and possibly stopped an earthquake in its tracks and now she was being forcibly dragged away by a stranger. She had to be going mad!

Walking into the park, Mirim didn't stop at the first bench they passed. It wasn't until they'd walked at least ten minutes in silence down a gravel path before she sat down. The further they walked the more agitated Kiera's mind became as it tried to escape Mirim's grasp.

Mirim sat and forced Kiera to sit beside her. She gently withdrew from Kiera's consciousness and began to speak rapidly.

"We'll be safe here. We'll be able to see if anyone comes along. You are not from this world. I can prove it." She added more slowly in a softer tone, "Do you have a green pendant or necklace?"

Nonplussed, Kiera stared wildly around. There was no one she could call for help. Sensing the other girl's distress, Mirim sent her thoughts back to Kiera soothing her as if she were a wild animal. She settled herself back on the bench and tried to make herself as non-threatening as possible and waited.

Calming down slowly, Kiera silently reached behind her white shirt and brought out the small green crystal her aunt had given her.

Mirim continued, "That represents the earth element. It belongs to the Terill family - your family. It focuses your power. I'm not an Earth element so I don't really know what you can do with it, but I do know that it is linked with nature. You can heal and you probably have an affinity with stones."

Strange as it was to hear this, Kiera had always known that she was different. She thought it was because of her traveler blood. She had heard of fortune-tellers in other groups, so she just assumed that her power was some sort of extension to that. She didn't really look like any of her family, she mused. It would explain why her father never paid her any attention - except when it profited him.

"OK, so if I am an earth element, what are you?" she asked.

"Air." Mirim replied. Reaching into her own shirt she brought out a silk purse and showed her own small crystal.

"We are opposites or complementary powers - depending on your point of view. Traditionally yours and my family were great friends."

"So what are we, priestesses or something?" Kiera asked.

"Huh, oh no. Our families, along with three others used to rule Eleria, our home world," Mirim explained. "Somehow, the Magi, I'll explain later, tricked their way into an Elementi stronghold and killed nearly all the ruling caste. There were five ruling families, the Firellis, Ariels, Aquels, Terills and the Omnax family. The eldest in the Omnax family is our High-King or Queen. The rest of the families are Kings and Queens of lesser domains. Each has a power. Your family has powers over earth and nature, mine air and sky, the Firelli had control over fire, and the Aquels water and the sea."

"What did the Omnax have?" Kiera interrupted.

"Spirit. While the crystals focus our power, the Omnax family can focus the combined power of everyone. Even our domains reflected the crystal structure. My family had the highlands, yours, the fertile plains; Firelli ruled the desert people and the Aquels, the islands and coastal regions."

"I don't understand why you didn't come looking for me before now?"

"I had to wait for the High-King to activate his power. Without him, I wouldn't be able to find you. You could have been anywhere in the universe, in any universe! You were sent a hundred years in the future to keep you safe. My great-grandmother had to stay behind to keep the Matrix working. It needs an Elementi mind in contact at all times to stay alive."

"Right, so that means you've already found the Omnax king or queen?"

"High-King." Mirim corrected her. "Yes, but he doesn't want anything to do with us."

Mirim's face twisted with frustration.

"It's his heritage! He thinks it is not his problem. It is his problem. While he lives, the Emperor must die. There can only be one person with that power and Aras is not the true heir. To live, Aras must send someone to kill him. I can't do it all alone. I need help. Will you help me?"

"One more question, how come I can

understand you? Surely if you are from another world you would be speaking another language?"

Mirim rubbed her forehead. She didn't have time for this!

"When we were children, although we can't remember it, we were given our crystals to touch. At the same time we were introduced to the Matrix. Our minds were keyed to the Matrix mind as heirs. Our language would have passed to you in that instant. Take a look at the skin between your thumb and index finger."

Kiera opened her left hand.

"No, sorry, I meant the other one." Mirim said.

Examining the skin, Kiera saw a pale section of skin she had not noticed before.

"That happens when people are keyed into the Matrix. The pigmentation is somehow corrupted. No matter how tanned you get, you will always have a pale shaped circle there." Mirim explained.

Kiera sat back thoughtful. There was nothing keeping her here. She planned to start a new life anyway. This was a new world Mirim was promising!

Decision made, Kiera replied "Yes, I think I will. Where do I sign up?"

Relieved, Mirim stood up. "It's better if you

stand up. The odds of teleporting to another seat are small. I fell over several times as a child when I tried that. I soon learned to stand!" As with Jake she showed Kiera how to access the Matrix. Together they 'ported to Jake's home.

They appeared by the same tree Mirim had rested against earlier. Mirim leant against Kiera.

"Are you all right?" Kiera asked.

"Yes" Mirim smiled weakly. "I just get really nauseous when I teleport."

Kiera touched Mirim on the arm and concentrated, "Better?"

Mirim stood up straight, shaking her head experimentally.

"I wish you were around earlier!"

"Which house is the one from the Omnax family?" asked Kiera looking around.

"His name is Jake, Kiera."

"What's he like?"

"He's clever. I picked that up from the meld." Mirim pointed at the intercom.

"Do you know how to use that box?"

"Sure." Kiera reached out to the box and pressed the button. It crackled for a moment and an impatient voice answered.

"Well, who is it?" A male voice barked.

Kiera raised an eyebrow. "Charming man."

Pressing the button again, Kiera replied "We'd like to speak to Jake please."

Nothing happened for a little while. Kiera was just about to try again. Maybe he hadn't heard her? They heard a door close. Jake ambled towards them, hands in pockets, hood raised to keep the chill off.

"Mirim, you found her!" he called from halfway down the path.

"Yes, her name is Kiera. Have you changed your mind?" Mirim called back.

"Not really. I suppose I could help you find the other elements though. It's Fire and Water next isn't it?"

"Have you tried searching for them yet on your own?" Kiera asked.

Jake laughed ruefully as he drew close.

"Well actually I did. I sensed some fire activity about half an hour ago but however hard I try, I can't sense any water. Could she be hiding near water?" Jake asked Mirim.

"Possibly, maybe if we search for the fire first we can use all our combined energy to find the water king."

Kiera looked confused. "You know water is a boy?"

"Oh, didn't I tell you?" They both shook their heads. "Oh, my great-grandmother recorded the names of the children they sent away. You were all imprinted on the Matrix. That is why it is so easy to connect to it.

"You all have different Elementi names. Jake," she pointed at the boy. "Your real name is Malo Omnax. Your mother named you after your father. Kiera," she pointed at the girl "you are Lessa Terill. The others are Dinar Firelli, a boy's name and Shey Aquel. Which could be a boy or girl's name, but is likely to be boy."

"Do you all want to come in?" Jake asked, rubbing his arms. "It's getting cold out here."

Mirim and Kiera nodded together. Noticing Kiera's backpack, Jake asked Mirim, "Didn't you bring any bags?"

Mirim looked embarrassed, "I didn't expect to be here that long." Jake shrugged and led the way up to the house.

"We'll have to be quiet," he said opening the front door. "Ben, my uncle, is back and he gets short-tempered at night."

Quietly they crept past the living room and up the two flights of stairs to Jake's room. Kiera didn't know what she would expect from the room of the next High-King but this was not it. Her eyes roamed the room.

On the left she identified a computer buried under piles of paper. Wading through the dirty clothes on the floor she perched on the end of the unmade bed. A TV was on in the corner - just visible over the frame of a bike. How?'

Following her gaze, Jake saw the bike. "Oh, they won't let me keep it downstairs overnight. I have to leave it outside or I bring it up here."

Mirim shook her head. "Can you turn that noise down?"

"Sure." Jake clambered over the bed.

"Wait!" Jake and Mirim turned to stare at Kiera, "What?"

"Listen! What they are saying on the news – look at that!"

'Reports have come in of a volcanic eruption on the small island of Vulcano in Italy. Five British tourists were killed among the hundreds reported dead. Experts say they are baffled by the eruption. The last recorded eruption was in 1890. There were no warning signs.

It ended as mysteriously as it started. Experts are predicting no further eruptions in the immediate future. Evacuations are taking place as a precaution. If anyone has any friends or relatives in the area, the Foreign and Commonwealth Service has set up a phone line...'

"That was me! I stopped that volcano!" Kiera said. "I felt a tremor and suddenly I was there - inside the volcano. It was amazing."

"That was about the time I felt the fire element used," Jake interjected.

"The earthquake didn't feel right. It was like someone had made it happen. It wasn't natural."

Mirim brushed her gold hair out of her eyes. Could Dinar Firelli have gone bad? The thought was too terrible to even think of. Who knew what kind of life he grew up with here? The fire element was the most volatile and the family tended to follow the pattern... but to cause a volcano? She had never heard of the family going that far.

Kiera and Jake looked at Mirim expectantly. Mirim sighed, "We have to find him and find out what happened. If he's gone mad we will have to stop him, somehow. If we can get him to the Citadel, maybe we can do something for him."

"Jake, do you have a map?"

"Sure." His voice sounded puzzled. He crossed over to where his computer desk stood. Reaching up to the shelves he pulled a large atlas out of its place. He moved towards the bed, kicking a pair of jeans as he offered it to Mirim. Mirim took it and flicked through it to find what she needed. The open page showed the entire globe flattened out. She motioned the other two to kneel beside her.

"Jake, get out your crystal and concentrate on what you felt when the volcano happened. Hang the crystal over the page. It should pull you to where he is. We'll help you."

Jake pulled the crystal from behind his t-shirt. It was glowing slightly, seemingly in anticipation. Placing it over the book, he channeled his awareness through the crystal. He felt Kiera and Mirim's consciousnesses join his own, in a small pyramid of power with his own mind the apex.

The crystal weaved across the page as if looking for where to go. As it hovered over the channel, he got a brief flash of water. Jake shook his head. Mirim's thought reached him, Concentrate! Moving the crystal over the water on the map, he felt the crystal motion change to a circular motion. "He's over the water. He's in the shape of a... bird?"

They could all see it now. It was a bird of prey with red and gold feathers. As they watched, it turned its head as if it sensed their attention.

Jake could hear Mirim gasp behind him. The bird ignored them and flew faster. Their vision kept pace and they saw it begin to writhe in the air. It was fighting something! The air around it shimmered and shone a brilliant white. A moment later and it was gone. There was nothing but the grey sky and sea.

The vision faded away, and all three collapsed on the floor with cramp.

"Next time we do this, I vote we sit in chairs," Kiera grumbled. She grabbed her crystal and healed herself first before hovering her hands over the other's calves.

Mirim didn't reply, deep in thought. Something wasn't right. She'd felt the energy ripples which only happened when teleporting through to another dimension. He couldn't travel on his own. Aras must have found a way to grab him.

She reached out to the Matrix. Deep in the Citadel the yellow crystals lit up as she connected. He hadn't used the power of the Citadel. He must have been taken! But to where? She entered the coordinates into the Matrix. Tracing the trail from Earth it led direct to Eleria. She gasped as she saw the final destination. Not only did he go to Eleria but the coordinates led right back to the old

Elementi castle!

Mirim withdrew smoothly back into her body. Jake had said he couldn't even get a glimmer of the water element. His power should be strong enough now that he should at least feel something. What if the heir never arrived on Earth? Her mother had said the power had failed on the last transfer. Their checks would have shown that he or she would not have been on Eleria at the time, but what if she were sent to the future Eleria - the Eleria of now? She had to get Jake and Kiera back. The other elements were back there now and for good or for worse she needed to reunite the powers - even if she had to lie. Decision made she turned to address Jake.

"I know you don't want to leave your life here, but why not come back with us, just for a visit? As soon as we find the others, we can send you back."

Jake nursed his ankle. Why not? It wouldn't take long. Hadn't they found Kiera in a day?

"OK."

Mirim waved her arm to grab their attention. "We all need to connect to the Matrix. Teleporting to another dimension is not like teleporting across the road. We need to really concentrate. That said, with the three of us we will have enough combined energy to create a portal.

"Jake, you need to take the lead. You go first, next Kiera and I'll take up the rear." Jake nodded. All three took out their crystals and enclosed them in their left hands. Following Mirim's lead, Jake took Kiera's left hand and Kiera took hold of Mirim's free hand.

Linked within a circle, all three concentrated on their crystals. Jake moved his awareness into the center of the circle. Spots of light danced between them creating a ball of light suspended several feet off the ground. Kiera joined Jake and the globe grew to almost fill the space between them. Mirim could make out the outline of the control room through the light. Lastly Mirim joined them, falling into the now familiar meld with ease. The light increased, covering the trio and imploded.

Karl climbed the tree grumbling under his breath. He hated climbing. His clothes were filthy and the rain was trickling down his cuffs soaking his sleeves. He'd called Jake three times since the beach. Each time it had gone straight to voicemail. Something was wrong.

Reaching out to the red slates his hand slipped on the wet tiles. His heart skipped a beat as he steadied himself against the old oak tree again. Breathing slowly through his nose and mouth, he made himself concentrate. He could hear voices floating down from Jake's room.

If only Ben would let him through the front door! Karl grunted as he grabbed hold of the guttering and swung himself up on to the sloping roof. He'd only scratched his car once and it was an accident! Karl ground his teeth at the memory.

The window sill was only an arm's length away and he was able to pull himself closer. His jaw dropped as he watched Jake and two figures through the streaming window. They were holding hands and a bright light formed between them. The light grew larger obscuring the figures from view.

Karl yanked the window open and jumped inside, He threw himself at the light to help his friend.

CHAPTER ELEVEN - ELERIA

It had taken Shenella more than an hour to get away from the emperor's apartment. The First Adviser's arrival with urgent business had interrupted them. Luckily, Aras had invited her to sit with him in the outer room. The First Adviser would never have dared enter the Emperor's inner chamber. Under the First Adviser's severe gaze she had backed away and slipped into the corridor while they were talking about her.

Leaving the room Shenella considered Aras's strange behavior. Marta must have done something to him - it was the only explanation. For the entire hour, Aras had stared soulfully into her eyes protesting that he was sorry. He wouldn't say for what, but she guessed. There was only one thing he would be sorry for. But why now? He had never shown any signs of remorse before - in the two years she had lived here.

Reaching the fork in the corridor she was about to turn right, back to her own apartment when she had second thoughts. Marta and Ecu would be at dinner now in the great hall. If she was going to find out what was going on, this would be the perfect opportunity to find out if there was anything incriminating in his apartment.

Turning left, she moved towards the west wing. The whole complex she recalled represented the Elements of the families that once lived here. She had left the center apartments where the High-King had lived. Her own apartment in the north of the complex had belonged to the Air family.

There had been no reason to go to this part of the castle before and she was unsure which of the doors led to Ecu's apartment. Approaching the last door she saw it was dusted recently. She felt a shiver of apprehension. *This had to be it.* She traced the outline of the fountain carved on the wood with her fingertips. She knocked quietly.

She hoped no one was in there. Hearing no

footsteps she dared to open the door a crack - the room behind was dark. Feeling more confident, she opened the heavy door wide enough to slip through. Careful to make sure the door didn't slam behind her, she gently pulled it closed.

She was in. She couldn't see much as her eyes adjusted but there was just enough moonlight to make out the shapes of the furniture and paintings against the wall. It seemed familiar somehow as if she had been here before. She knew this was impossible. This side of the castle had only reopened the year before. As more representatives arrived they needed more space for the myriad kingdoms that had sprung up since the decline of the old Elementi Empire.

As if in a dream, she moved to the window. It was a cloudless night and the view of the city was spectacular. The old grand public buildings stood tall over the squat homes of the merchant class. Even at this time of night people scurried to and fro like ants beneath her. In the distance she could see the stone wall marking the edge of the original city and farther still the Eastern plains where the Earth Queen had once ruled. Squinting her eyes she could just make out the bonfires of the nomads in the distance. By morning there would be no trace of them. Their fires were an act of defiance against the people they believed had killed their queen-goddess. She shook her head. The days of the Elementi were over - no matter what Ecu had said.

Shenella turned back to the room, on her right was a mural. Intellectually she knew she should be looking for something to do with Ecu but she felt drawn to the picture. Closer now, she could make out an underwater city, probably based on one of the Merpeople cities.

On the bottom right was a painted gold chest. It was so realistic she couldn't help touching the lock on it - she felt something give. Confused she pressed harder. She heard the sound of a lock click. Where the chest had been, a small door was now open. Reaching inside she pulled out a little bundle wrapped in muslin. Curious to see what was in it she unwrapped the parcel carefully. Inside was a small blue crystal.

Holding it up to the light it reflected the moonlight as well as hold it. It was so beautiful. Tiny pinpricks of light crashed against each other, some flowing slowly and others jumping together in an eternal random pattern, hypnotizing her with its beauty. A small part of her that she did not realize was empty was suddenly filled. She let go of all her inhibitions, thoughts, feelings, everything as she stared into the depths of the crystal. She was filled with a happiness she had not felt for a very long time.

In her mind's eye pictures began to form. A woman was pacing the room. She was waiting for someone. She was dressed in blue finery, blue dress, blue jewelry...

A man came to the door, she saw him take off a crystal from around his neck. He wrapped it in muslin and placed it in the hiding place she found in the wall. Taking the woman's arm he moved to escort her out. The woman paused, reached down and picked up a child sitting on the rug. Giving it a kiss on the cheek, she set it down again. Somehow, Shenella knew she was that child.

The woman smiled tenderly and followed the man out leaving her alone. No, there was someone else there. Shenella focused on the figure standing by the child. It was blurry. It rippled and she saw it was made of water. She remembered. An Ashrey! It was her nanny. Her mind stalled, she didn't want to think what happened next. It had looked after her after...

She remembered now, the Ashrey had taken her away. Something bad had happened. She sighed as the memory eluded her. The next thing she remembered was being placed in what she supposed must have been her foster parent's arms.

Lost in her memories, she didn't hear the door open. Hearing it slam she spun around to find Ecu looking at her. She must have been here too long. But he wasn't staring at her; she followed his gaze to her hand. He was looking at the crystal! Protectively she held it closer.

Taking her chance she skirted the table to her right and dashed out into the light of the corridor. She heard his heavy footsteps follow her out of the room. Panicking she instinctively made herself invisible and ran. When she was sure he wasn't behind she slowed down, craning her neck behind to make sure. As she did, she crashed into something. To her horror, it was the Mer Ambassador.

At the force of the impact she remembered. He could see her, even when she was invisible.

"I'm sorry sir. Please excuse me" she mumbled.

"Wait just a moment there. Why are you in such a rush?" But he was not looking at her. Just as Ecu's had done, his eyes were drawn to the crystal glowing softly in her hand.

"A crystal." He breathed. He dropped to his

knees, "My queen."

"What, I'm no queen. Not yet, anyway."

Sori looked up into the frightened girl's eyes. She might be his queen but she didn't know who she was. He'd better get her out of here he thought. If he recognized the crystal and what it meant someone else probably would as well.

Taking her hand gently, he asked. "Do you trust me? Use the crystal - look into my heart and mind. I wish you no harm, but I need to get you out of here." He drew her towards the back staircase.

"Can you extend your shield? Can you make me invisible as well?"

Shenella nodded. She hadn't tried it before but she knew it could be done. She imagined herself in a tight shield as she had done a hundred times before. She extended the shield outwards until it covered Sori as well.

Rounding the corner, they passed some dignitaries talking to one another earnestly. They didn't spare the duo a look. If they had seen them they would have certainly called the guards. As the Emperor's chosen consort any man's touch on Shenella was a hanging offence.

Moving swiftly now, confident that Shenella's

shield was strong enough, Sori opened the door into the kitchens. He expertly dodged the serving girls and boys as they prepared the kitchen for the next day. Passing through to the room beyond, Sori mentally called for his guard to get ready his coach. Their only hope was to get to the sea as soon as possible.

He would not be missed but even though Shenella thought she was ignored, her absence from the evening's entertainment would be soon noted. His ambassadorial status would mean nothing.

As he entered the carriage, Sori wondered if he was doing the right thing. With both Shenella and himself gone, it would be construed as an act of war. Aras would not hesitate to mobilize his forces against his people. That his father would not be pleased was a gross understatement. But when his father realized whom he had with him...

The coach moved rapidly west through the city to the docks. Shenella sat silently opposite Sori. She was inwardly trying to digest what she had learnt. She wasn't Shenella Berek. Her whole life was a sham. She was young when her 'foster' parents had taken over her care but even then she had known her name was Shey

Aquel.

She must have only been around three years old but she recalled her tantrums when the Bereks had tried to instill in her the new name. Her parents must have been terrified that someone would find out.

She reflected miserably that it was to no avail. No one found out and still they died because of who she was. She felt tears hot against her cheeks.

Sori handed her a handkerchief in understanding silence. He knew her story. It could have been no other way. The collective conscience of his people remembered the day the King died as if they had suffered the same fate themselves. They had felt the sharp pain of the sword as it had taken the life they almost worshipped.

They thought the family was dead. They couldn't feel the element's presence for so long that they believed the whole family must have died. The power of the crystal was a throbbing in the back of his consciousness. He'd never felt it before but he knew what it meant. Now he knew the truth. The Ashrey must have been able to transport her into the future somehow. If a remnant of this family was alive perhaps the others had managed to escape. A small flame of hope kindled inside him.

The carriage soon bumped over the rough cobbles at the approach to the docks. Sori sat up straighter. Shenella was too new to her powers to be able to travel to the city underwater. They would need to charter a ship.

Meanwhile, in the castle, Ecu's mind was buzzing. That had been the Water King's amulet! He'd seen it in engravings at the library. After losing the girl he went straight to the Emperor's quarters begging an audience. At first he was turned away by one of Aras' guards - but he had persisted and after waiting only a half-hour gained an audience with an irritable Aras.

"My Lord, Shenella is the Water Queen!"

"Don't be stupid, what are you blithering about man. The Water King died nearly a hundred years ago. Is this what you woke me up to tell me?"

Ecu paused; he'd better tread carefully. Aras was not the fearful man his father had been but he could still order a death at the drop of a heral - especially as he could see the signs of him suffering another of his headaches.

He changed tact.

"Your Highness, I returned from dinner to find

Shenella in my apartments." Aras' face clouded with anger.

Speeding up, Ecu continued, "Sire, I was given the apartments of the old Water King. I returned this evening and I found Shenella in the outer room holding a crystal. She seemed to be in some sort of trance. I started to say something and she ran away. I tried to chase her but she was too quick."

The anger drained from Aras' face but he still looked skeptical.

"Shenella? She has been here for a couple of years now and I haven't seen any evidence of power. Never mind the old power."

"That was it." Ecu said excited. "She looked so startled. I am sure she does not even know what and who she is. She probably used her magic unconsciously without thinking, to hide herself. You never noticed her around much did you?"

Thoughtfully Aras shook his head. It was strange. He had gone to a lot of effort to track her down. He'd first seen her with her parents in the city. He never left the castle much but on that day, one of his nobles had insisted that he go for a ride with him for exercise. After a particularly bad Council session, he had agreed.

As soon as he saw her, he knew Shenella was

different. Most of his nobles brought their daughters to him in the hope he would choose one of them to be his bride. He had learned to avoid most of these situations but had taken up the offer of the ride to clear his head after the particularly exhaustive meeting. He'd passed her as he rode out of the city on his way to the plains.

Most of the daughters he was presented with had dark hair and skin. She was blond. Only a few of the old people had blond hair and almost none of the Magi had. It was a novelty. He remembered thinking that it was strange at the time - that her parents both had dark hair, but he had just brushed the thought aside.

He'd wanted her for his wife the first time he saw her. The Emperor should have the best of everything, the most beautiful, the unusual. Her green eyes captivated him. He'd only seen her for a moment as they rode past but he had obsessed about her for days afterwards.

The next morning he had sent several agents into the city. His most faithful brought back news of who she was within hours. His First Adviser had counseled vehemently against it. She was of the old people. He advised him to choose a daughter of the Magi Council, but he'd refused and ordered the First Adviser to get him the girl at all costs.

She had arrived at the castle a couple of months later. She'd obviously been crying and she looked frailer than he remembered. He left her alone; he knew she was his. It wasn't as if she was going anywhere, she was one of his possessions - to be ignored until she came of age and he needed her.

So she was gone. Not only that, but now she was a threat. She was living proof the Elementi children had escaped. He needed to think this over.

"You may go." He told Ecu.

"But Sire, we must get her. If nothing else, I must study her. She was able to use her powers without any thought. We have to train years to use ours. Furthermore, what about her crystal? Wouldn't you like that? With your white power you could use it when it would be deadly for any of us to even hold it."

Aras looked at the older man thoughtfully. "I will think on it; now go!" Defeated Ecu backed off and left the room.

At the harbor Sori was haggling with a captain.

"...five herals for the two of us."

"What about your guards?"

"They'll make their own way there. I need you to take us to Pumar Island off the Drata coast."

"I know where Pumar is. I will take ten herals and that my friend is my final offer, five for each of you. You're obviously in a hurry and no one leaves this late unless they are in some sort of trouble. I'm the only captain leaving for at least two days. If you need to leave now you are going to have to take my offer."

Sori blinked and hid his smile. He brought out his money pouch and counted the coins firmly into the other man's hand. He'd expected to pay twice that. Once the captain was satisfied he moved aside to let the two pass on to the ship.

The captain didn't know what to make of these two. As he watched, the lady's cape blew in the wind. Her hand reached up swiftly to pull the hood over her head but it was too late and the captain saw the rare combination of green eyes and blonde hair. He stifled a gasp. There was bound to be more than one girl like that. Still, he'd better get moving. He called out to his first mate.

Shenella made her way to the stern of the ship. As the ship slowly left the harbor, Sori joined her.

"Do you know who you are?"

She nodded. She was young when her real parents died but she now knew everything that three-year-old did. The feeling of loss was as if it had happened just yesterday and in a sense it had. As she gazed into the crystal she had felt the emotions of that three year-old's mind. She had felt the happiness and feeling of safety in her mother's arms. The fear and pain as her father died and the confusion as she was taken by her Ashrey nurse.

She didn't understand how she could be here though. That was a hundred years ago or as near to as made no difference. Sori guessed what was troubling her.

"You're wondering how you came to be in the future? I can make an educated guess at that."

He rubbed his chin. "None of the children were ever found. There was always the hope that you had escaped, but until now it was only that - a hope. There was an heir to all the families at the time except for the Omnax family. However, from that little show the other day - even that is in doubt now. If they all escaped... if it is true that the High-King had an heir that escaped - the Elementi circle can be reborn. There is a chance that Eleria can be at peace again."

Shenella wrapped her cloak tighter around

her to protect her from the sharp breeze. As they pulled further from shore the breeze began to grow colder. She didn't know what to think. She was on the boat, and she was alive. She didn't know the stranger but she knew deep down that he was safe. She supposed it was the crystal. It seemed to be almost talking to her. If she concentrated she felt like it was trying to enter her mind. That if she only let go she would discover something incredible. She was scared.

Sori stepped back. Shenella wasn't responding. He decided to leave her alone for a while; she probably just needed some time to think over everything. Her whole world had been turned upside down.

He knew a little about her supposed history. Her parents had died in a carriage accident a couple of years ago. Her guardians who he heard were in the pockets of the emperor had brought her to the castle. He supposed she didn't go willingly. Even that was a lie, she found out today the mother and father she grew up with weren't even her parents. He could feel some of the turmoil she was feeling. There was nothing he could do for her at present. He needed to take her home. She wouldn't be completely safe but it was the best place for her now.

There would be war over this, but her power could be enough to ensure the autonomy of his, no, their people. For the chance to overthrow the Magi's influence in the islands - it would be worth it.

He melted into the darkness and headed back to the cabin. They should reach their destination by morning and hopefully a brighter future.

CHAPTER TWELVE - PURSUIT

Aras was furious, of all the ungrateful... They wouldn't get away with this! The urge to smash something was strong, his hands clenched and unclenched as he battled with his anger. The servants standing nearby froze, unwilling to make a noise and become the outlet. With no obvious available target, Aras took some deep breaths and managed to restrain the urge. He should have paid more attention to the girl. She had been given far too much freedom!

"Guards!" he shouted. Two guards by the door rushed to his side.

"Send some men to find the girl and the Ambassador." They didn't move immediately, his head whipped around.

"Now!" he barked. They jumped and ran out

almost tripping over themselves in their hurry.

Aras was never good at waiting and the whole castle knew it. As he moved to sit back down on his throne, the courtiers quietly left one by one, each intent on finding something else to do, somewhere else to be.

Hours later the last guard to come back entered the hall cowering. Aras stood on the dais, his face impassive giving nothing away. The other messengers were already lined up on the right, their eyes fixated on the wall opposite. To provoke his anger in this mood would probably mean their death.

The last messenger was a small man – surprisingly so, Aras thought. He was surprised he had made it past the height restriction to even get in his guard. Aras saw with contempt the man's gaze was pointed at the ground, refusing to meet his eyes. Coward! Anger welled up inside him sending his fury to new heights. There was no need to guess the man had not found the fugitives.

Hesitantly looking up, the man began to speak.

"Lord, the ship had gone by the time I got there. There was nothing I could do. I asked at the port but there won't be another ship until the tide turns. The Admiralty said it wouldn't be safe to go through the straits until tomorrow."

Aras' eyes flashed, "You lost them?" his voice was dangerously low.

"We know where they went!" the man quickly interjected. "A beggar saw a couple beg passage on to a ship. They meet the description. They asked the Captain to take them to Pumar."

Aras stormed out of the hall. He headed for the ante-room and slammed the door as he thundered through. It was time to talk to Adramelech.

Once in the secret room, he paused to calm down. He knew never to contact another being while not in full control. He leant on the table nearest the door, his head in his arms. He concentrated on his breathing. His heartbeat gradually slowed. He felt betrayed and now it was time to act.

Once he was sure he was calm enough he strode to the edge of the painted circle. Clasping his hands in front of him he began to murmur the words that would bring the fire-being under his control. After a few minutes he felt the pressure in the air alter imperceptibly. His voice rose.

"Adramelech, I command you to return." He all but shouted. A burst of fire illuminated the circle - he caught a brief glimpse of a bird like shape and Adramelech was there.

"Why have you called me now!"

"I was about to ask you why you have not killed the boy-king yet!"

The creature's eyes glowed red. "I was about to get to him when you pulled me here, stupid human."

Aras flinched. Twisting his finger, he muttered some arcane words in a low voice. The creature writhed, its red flames turning yellow blue. The creature screamed in pain.

"While you are in my circle you would be wise to show respect," Aras snarled. *While I may be losing control of his court, I can still master this creature*, he thought with satisfaction.

Adramelech howled in impotent rage. How dare this human threaten him? The human need only show just one weakness and he would...

Aras screamed, his head! He clutched it forgetting about all else. He could hardly see. The pressure was intense. It felt like it was about to explode. His concentration broke for a moment. His grasp of the force field faltered, and it collapsed. Adramelech roared. He was free! The Deoc leapt out of his temporary prison in glee. Now was his chance. The demon readied himself to pounce, tensing his thoughts to devour the human's energy, but a stray thought stopped him. He swiveled his head.

Why had the circle broken? The boy? The boy was here! - In Eleria! Adramelech turned his attention back to Aras cowering on the floor. He cackled, who was in charge now? He touched the man on his forearm, branding him with fire. Never again would he be able to control him. The creature took one more look at his pathetic opponent and disappeared. He would deal with him later.

Shenella landed on Pumar with mixed feelings. She had never been to the islands before. She knew it was a popular tourist spot but her family had never left their estates other than to visit the city. Her father had always said, "Why buy glass when you already have crystal?" He didn't know what he was missing, Shenella thought.

She was amazed at the differences. She wouldn't say people in the city were unhappy, but here... the very air seemed to be lighter, happier. The few people in the harbor she saw all wore bright dyes as if the sunny colors on their clothes reflected in their natures.

Sori had explained on the ship that Pumar was just a stopping off point and they still had a fair way to go. She was fascinated by these people and had begged to explore just for a half-day. Sensing her need to get away for a while, Sori acquiesced reluctantly. Now he had met her and touched her mind he knew he would be able to find her anywhere on Pumar. He would sense it if she got into trouble.

The path to the village was short but she decided to take it slow to enjoy the breath-taking scenery. She had grown up in the mountains of the highlands so she had never been deprived of good views. The snow-peaked mountains during midwinter were particularly beautiful but there was something about the sea that called her. She wasn't sure if it was the sound of the waves crashing against the surf or merely the sense of freedom she felt when it was impossible to tell where the sea ended or sky began.

She still found it difficult to accept she was the Water Queen. She smiled - no wonder she loved being beside the sea. Why hadn't it occurred to her to visit the port in the city before?

The gravel crunched underfoot as she trudged up the steep path. The sun felt gloriously hot on her back and the sounds of the birds calling to each other only served to make her even more at peace. In just a few minutes she stopped to rest. Her wanderings around the castle were no preparation for climbing a cliff. Stretching her arms above her head, she twisted, and straightened her spine, taking in the panorama below her. The ship was on its way out. In the distance she could see the sailors as they ran around the deck of the ship like an army of worker ants. Her gaze switched to the beach. She searched for Sori; he must have rounded the cliff to the right. Shenella shrugged. He said he needed to see someone who lived there. Climbing again, she resolved to just enjoy herself. There was still most of the morning left to explore. He would find her when he needed her.

A strange grove of oak trees was ahead of her. Curious, she stepped off the path to have a closer look. Getting nearer she could see that the grove must have some religious significance. She remembered reading about the old gods in a book of mythology in her parents' library. She was in the islands so they probably worshipped some sort of water god or goddess. Her memory of the book was a little hazy on the subject but if she remembered right, the gender of the royalty in power affected the deity worshipped. Maybe they'll worship me? She giggled at the blasphemous idea.

The grove of trees was set in a semicircle around a low stone altar. The shade cast shadows on her cheeks as she walked through the nearest trees. Their symmetry was lovely. As she examined the altar, she noticed some fresh fruit had recently been laid there in a woven basket. Interesting, she was sure the Empire had stamped out such worship. Someone had been here recently. Perhaps the grove was all part of the tourist trek.

She considered staying there for the morning, since it was so peaceful, but she didn't know when she would be able to come back to the island. Having been cooped up in the castle for so long she wanted to explore!

Shenella pushed on and re-joined the path to the village. She had heard some of the nobles discussing the village after their trips. Her cheeks colored. If she ever needed proof that she was invisible to them, those conversations were it.

Reaching the clearing at the center of the village she saw it also doubled as a busy market. She wove through the stalls, picking up and putting down small local crafts. Tired after her brief walk, Shenella bought a drink at the first stall that sold refreshments. Settling into a brightly covered chair, she crossed her ankles and picked up her drink.

She was still there watching an argument with a stallholder and an awkward local when Sori arrived at midday. They were making a scene. The customer's voice was far too high-pitched for the size of the man.

Shenella's blond hair spilled over the back of the chair she was sitting on. Her eyes were half-open and her face was relaxed into a smile. At least she was smiling, Sori thought - a definite improvement on the morning. Slipping into the seat next to her, he languidly put his legs up on the chair opposite.

"Enjoying the show?" he enquired.

Shenella laughed. "These people are very different from the city people aren't they?"

"Well, of course. The city is only a small part of the Empire. There is a whole world out there." Sori's voice lowered in earnest. "We need to get to the underwater city soon. It is the only place you will be safe. The Emperor has the old High-King's blood and magic in him. He may be able to search for you through your magic, but the sheer weight of water above the city should disguise your power. It is getting stronger by the way, even since we met. I can feel it."

"I know, it's since I found the crystal. Something else happened a couple of hours ago. I don't know what it was. It was as if the very air changed. It seemed charged somehow."

Sori frowned. "I don't know what that would be. We need to swim from here to get to the underwater city. There is no other way of getting us there safely. It is impossible to charter a boat or ship to take us there directly. It is forbidden to go there any other way."

"How far is it?"

"A few miles."

"Wh-a-a...?"

Sori chuckled softly. "To do this I need to show you how to use your crystal to breathe underwater. Do you trust me?"

"Of course, you know I do. I wouldn't have gone this far with you if I didn't." she replied.

Sori stood up and held out his hand. "Come with me."

It was a lot quicker getting back to the beach than it had been walking to the village. The ship had gone of course by the time they got back to the deserted beach. Shenella looked up at the sky. The weather was taking a turn for the worse; she could see steely grey clouds coming closer in the distance. The water was calm now, but she wasn't sure how long it would stay that way.

Barefoot, Sori walked into the water. He beckoned for Shenella to join him. Taking off her silk shoes she left them out of reach of the water on the beach and picked up her skirts. Cautiously she picked her way over the sand, avoiding small stones and sharp shells until she was ankle deep in salt-water standing beside him.

"It's difficult for me to explain," Sori began. "Our people can live under the sea instinctively. We don't have to think about it, we just do it. We can breathe underwater because we have gills under our arms. We also produce a small electrical charge that we can extend a few millimeters away from our bodies. That keeps our clothes dry, if we wish."

"To be able to breathe underwater you will need to metamorphose your body to have the gills. That's what the old royalty used to do." Sori pulled one side of his shirt up showing her what they looked like.

Shenella took out her crystal. Taking comfort from Sori's small smile of encouragement, she concentrated on the jewel. Nothing happened. Frustrated she glanced up again at Sori.

"Have patience Shenella, I would have been surprised if you got it straight away. Concentrate on the crystal and imagine the gills on your skin."

She concentrated on its depths again. This time there were answering lights swirling like currents in the sea. She suddenly understood what she had to do. She needed to believe that she had gills - that she would be able to breathe underwater - to trust in the power.

Moving away from Sori, she walked deeper out and lay down until the water covered every part of her. Moments later her lungs burned as her body fought for breath, she refused to breathe through her nose and mouth. Her eyes closed in concentration. With that, it happened. Her skin felt as though it was tearing as gills formed under her arms. The pain lasted only for a moment before they opened and suddenly she could breathe. She twirled in the water, enjoying the feel of the current against her face.

Startled, she unexpectedly heard a voice in her mind.

'*That wasn't so hard was it?*'

How was this possible? In the murky water,

she couldn't see Sori but she knew he was close.

'Come on we need to go further in. It will take you a while to get used to the gloom.'

'How are we talking?' she asked.

'Mind to mind. There is no other way of talking in the ocean. If you tried talking with your mouth it would soon fill with water.' She could hear his laughter in her mind.

Bristling, she followed the direction of his thought-speech. After a while, she could see clearer. Schools of glittering fish swam alongside them for a few moments before they were replaced by another of a different color. They were surrounded by life. *'They know who you are Shenella; they can feel the old power in you.'*

Tucked safely in her shirt she could feel the crystal glowing gently against her skin in response. This was where her power was coming from. The life around her was somehow charging her crystal. She could feel it. She closed her eyes, sensing them with her mind.

There were millions of minds all around her, pinpoints of energy going for hundreds if not thousands of miles around. The sheer expanse of the sea astounded her. She never dreamed of such an amazing place.

Mechanically she swam, using the crystal's power to ease the way, trailing behind Sori's mental pattern through the ocean. It seemed like hours to Shenella before they were near the city. After the first few minutes in the ocean, she closed her eyes. Sori chided her but she insisted on keeping them closed. What she could see was too confusing against her mental image. The sea was too immense to take in all at once. It was easier to concentrate on Sori with only one sense.

Effortlessly she kept pace with him, the energy around her buoying her own and it was her power that let her know when they were nearing the city of the Merpeople.

Opening her eyes, she gasped. Sori must have sent a message ahead to let the Merpeople know they were coming. They were drifting at the bottom of a deep canyon. Steep rocks walls rose on each side creating a highway beneath them. Either side were caves carved in the hard rock. People stood in doorways and windows curiously watching their arrival. The water felt warmer here she realized. They must be near some natural hot springs.

A small reception committee stood near the end of the canyon. Sori and Shenella changed direction to swim towards them.

'*What is everyone wearing?*' Shenella asked Sori. Instead of the clothes worn at court that she was used to, they wore short or tight-fitting outfits. They were all green and made of some strange material she had not seen before.

'*They weave them from sea grass.*' he replied. '*If you'd had your eyes open you would have seen the meadows just past the island!*'

As they neared the small group of people, Shenella grew more and more nervous. Sensing her distress, Sori took hold of her hand and squeezed it.

'*It's all right; the one at the front is my father, the Kinar, our king. The rest are all his advisers. They are elected by the people.*'

The Kinar stepped forward.

'*Welcome to our city, my lady. My name is Chero and these are my advisers.*' He pointed to the surrounding men and women.

'*You must be tired. Sori will take you to the old Water King's apartments here. I trust you will find them comfortable.*'

Sori tapped her on the shoulder and pointed up the cliff face. The apartments were at the top. Baffled she kicked her legs and allowed him to escort her up.

'*They don't waste time with words do they?*'

'*My father hates unnecessary chatter. He is a very serious man. Don't worry, not everyone is like him. I'm not.*' Sori let go of her hand and pushed open a curtain of sea grass at the entrance.

As they stepped over the threshold her eyes widened in amazement. Evidence of sea grass was everywhere, from the bed and bedding to the curtains against the small window beside them. Seeing light in the far corner, she went to explore. There was a small corridor leading to a sitting room with plants on opposite walls. Each plant gave off a soft green or blue light creating a soothing ambience. It was beautiful.

Half-floating, half-walking towards the bedroom she saw Sori had turned on a light in there also. As she neared she was surprised to find a purple snail in a glass bowl. Its shell was a luminous royal purple merging into orange on the outer circle of its shell. Its glow was enough to light the whole room.

'*Is it all right?*' she asked.

'*Of course, if you want it to go dark just cover the bowl with this. You must remember to put food in there every day or they don't last long.*' He handed her a cloth.

'*Thank you, Sori - for everything.*'

'*My Lady, it was a pleasure and if you need*

anything, just let me know. I will pick you up for breakfast in the morning. Sweet dreams, my queen.' He smiled, touched her cheek, and floated out.

CHAPTER THIRTEEN - CITADEL

As soon as the light faded, Mirim broke away from the circle and dove through the doorway to the control room. Bemused, Kiera and Jake followed as she frantically swung her crystal back and forth over the glowing colored consoles. The white, green and yellow crystals were all glowing but to her evident surprise so was the blue. Frowning, she moved nearer. She was right. The Water Queen had never left Eleria.

As she stood back to take it in, the red panel began to glow a soft red. Jake and Kiera behind her joined her with questioning eyes. "They've all been used," she answered. "Earth, Fire, Air and Water - every element is activated. The red is not as bright which suggests Dinar was able to use his power without the crystal, so it was enough for the Matrix to pick up but no more. This is proof that all the families still exist and we can defeat the Magi!"

"Who are the Magi?" A voice unfamiliar to Mirim asked. She whirled, a boy she had never seen before stood in the doorway.

"Wha-a, Wh-o-o" her chin jerked back in surprise.

"Karl! How did you get here?" Jake asked.

"I don't know, I followed you into some light."

Mirim looked at Jake and the other boy and made the connection.

"Wonderful, a Terran. He'll only get in the way."

Jake ignored Mirim, "Karl, it's great to see you but you have to go back. It's too dangerous here."

"Where is here?" Karl asked his cool grey eyes taking in the bare white walls and the control crystals in the center of the room. He walked over to get a better look. Mirim sidled in front of him to block his way.

"We are in Eleria and you shouldn't be here."

"Well, if Jake is here I'm staying."

Jake grinned at his friend. "You know I want you here but it is too dangerous. I'll come back tomorrow."

"Well," Mirim interjected. They both looked at her.

"You can't go home."

"What! You told us we could!"

"I'm sorry I lied. Well, I didn't exactly lie but when I left to go to Earth I knew there was enough power for two trips at the most. I used so much power finding you and teleporting to Kiera that it used up all the power that we had. It will take a couple of months to produce enough power to go back."

"Great!" Jake threw his hands up in the air.

"I'm sorry, but the fate of the world is far more important than just getting back to your boring life."

"Not to me!"

Mirim looked at Jake's furious face for a moment before concentrating on the console again, choosing to ignore what he said. She stepped across to the blue crystals.

"The water element." She held her crystal closer. "It was used quite recently." Mirim frowned, losing herself in the complex information she was analyzing. "Here! She used it here!" Jake and Kiera jumped at her outburst.

"Sorry, I mean it was used above ground. A

few miles to the east are the islands. I think they are where Jersey is in your world. It shows the power was used there... but I can't trace her now. She must be either on or under water. Power protects its own. All I can say is that she is near where the Merpeople live. If she is by water she is safe from Aras for now."

"What about Karl?" Jake demanded.

"There's nothing we can do - just look at the white crystals!"

Jake threw an apologetic glance at Karl as he crossed over to the white crystals in the center.

"These are my crystals?"

Mirim took a mental step back. She had lived here her whole life. It was strange to think of the crystals belonging to anyone but herself.

"I suppose so."

Jake reluctantly pulled his own crystal out. "Can you show me how to use this? Maybe I can track the fire element? You told me the white crystals are connected to the rest. It makes sense that maybe I can help?"

Mirim exhaled a long slow breath. It was worth a go. Shey would be all right but they didn't know about Dinar. On impulse she tried to enter Jake's mind. It would be quicker to show him than tell him. Her thoughts sought his. Jake instinctively raised his barriers as he recognized the feather-light touch of her mind. She sought a way around. He would be stronger than her, the others presence would be adding to his power. His barriers were strong she had to give him that.

Unaware of the struggle, Kiera made as if to say something to Jake but changed her mind. It was enough to distract him. Mirim broke through his barriers and placed the false memory in - showing him how to use his crystal to track the fire element. Jake blinked and glared at her.

"Shouldn't you ask before you do that?"

Mirim blushed with embarrassment. Caught out in front of the others with one of the most basic rules of the Elementi, She'd spent too long on her own.

Jake was surprised to find connecting to the Matrix wasn't like earlier. Before it was more like requesting the information, now he was going to have to fully integrate with it.

Armed with the new knowledge, Jake took the plunge. Holding out his crystal, he held his awareness out towards the white crystals before him. He floated there bodiless for a moment and the Matrix grabbed him. His mind swirled in crystal. There were memories here, thousands of them. Lives of men and women going back hundreds of years swamped his senses, he struggled against the tide. Jake tried to orient himself, to become the dominant mind. However, it was too strong. He let go of his sense of self to become part of the pattern.

He saw the planet of Eleria as an organic computer. The planet's surface was a huge motherboard, a base for the Matrix symbiotic mind. Each individual crystal contributed to its memory. The minds of himself, Kiera, Mirim and almost everyone on the world provided the processing power. He was amazed at how everything was connected. Energy was coming from everywhere, from the natural volcanoes, to the plant life in the sea, from the tides to the winds - it all contributed. He saw the Matrix would endure forever but for one thing; it needed at least one of the Elementi to give it the spark of life.

His... no, their memories now spanned thousands of years to the first meeting of minds. He recalled the first day, the surprise at the first flicker of consciousness. There had been nothing and all of a sudden it had a mind - it could think.

Jake recalled the touch of the first alien minds as they fused with the Matrix mind. He felt their relief at finding a compatible uninhabited world and the fear that they may be too late. He found out that his people had come from a different dimension. It was Earth! Before arriving here, they had lived beside a volcano for centuries using it as a means of powering their city. Their civilization had become incredibly advanced but so dependent on their location that they moved their entire city across dimensions to escape its destruction.

In clear images he saw the first explorers arrive in a cave off one of the islands. They had used it as a base of operations, living there in a makeshift camp for a couple of years while they analyzed the planet.

Finding no indigenous life they moved the entire city. It took ten years of preparation but only ten minutes to transport it. For the entire first year of the preparations they had lived in the cave before building temporary houses above ground.

In time they had children. Jake couldn't help but feel for them. They were able to do things that before would have been impossible. The children could forecast the weather, find metals to mine or read minds. These children were able to hide it at the beginning but as they got stronger it became more difficult. The Elders of the city found out and cast them out. Even with all their science, they were still afraid of what they didn't understand.

The children were called freaks and worse. Jake felt their distress as if it was happening now. The crystals recorded emotions as well as memories. Ostracized by their families and neighbors, they had to leave and build a life away from everything they had known.

Forty years passed in a blink of an eye, he saw the original civilization begin to die. The planet wasn't as compatible as they first thought. Something prevented them from having children. Eventually the city lights grew dim.

The children of the caves as they became known were the only people left. Those caves, Jake realized were where it all began - it had somehow changed the parents but made the children adaptable to the world. Evolution at work, Jake recognized.

In his mind's eye, the pictures became clearer as the Matrix bonded fully with the humans. He saw the city die and the children forget. The civilization soon reverted to feudalism; the strongest and the most powerful became the leaders while the weakest were reduced to slavery. At the back of their minds the Matrix dwelt and grew until it was able to make contact.

It drew five children with the greatest talents and the cleverest minds back to the cave. Without knowing why they each took a crystal from the hundreds littering the floor. Their minds inexplicably fused with the crystals creating an unbreakable link with the Matrix mind.

It showed them how to find the abandoned city, taking them through a disused path from one of the nearest islands. They returned to their families and brought them to live in the city. A hundred years later they emerged once again into the world. A powerful combination was born, Atlantean science mixed with Matrix technology - the Elementi.

As the images died, Jake once again concentrated on the feel of power that would link him to the last member of the Firelli family. Finding the thread, he tweaked it until the sound of the vibrations filled his senses. Floating out of his body he moved upwards away from the Citadel. He quickly passed the upper floors and noted the Spartan interiors until he reached the outer wall. The force-field prickled his awareness as he went through, breaking into the water of the ocean. A matter of moments and he was out under the cloudless night sky.

In the Control Room Jake's body collapsed. Karl leapt forward.

"What's wrong with him?" He demanded.

Mirim rolled her eyes.

"Nothing, he's just out of his body. He'll come back."

"You could have at least warned him to sit down! What kind of person are you?"

Mirim ignored him.

Rotating slowly in the air Jake tried to locate the now familiar feel of the Fire element. It wasn't there. Confused he looked up the coordinates of where the power was last used. Finding them quickly, he focused on the numbers and sped towards them, letting the Matrix guide him.

He sped over the water only slowing down when he reached a port. Passing over he could see small fishing boats teeming with fish. People were running to and fro carrying huge baskets of the fish on to dry land, while still larger nets of fish were hauled on to the docks with ropes.

Passing the port he carried on through. This was Naven, he recalled from the Matrix meld, the capital city of Eleria. It wasn't a large city, he noted, not compared to London or even Cardiff or Edinburgh, but as there were no roads and motorways it left plenty of room for more buildings. The tallest houses were just three stories high. The shorter ones nearest the port were made of wood, the grander houses further in were made out of some local yellow stone.

To the right of the city lay the castle. Settling on a rooftop a few streets away, Jake paused. It was not safe to go any further. How would the fire element have survived in the Magi stronghold? It didn't make sense.

He reached out for the vestiges of the Fire Element again. It wasn't there now. If the fire element was on earth and Aras had grabbed him, he would have been taken here for sure. According to the schematics the Matrix held, there were prisons underneath. If he were able to use enough power to make the console glow, maybe he would have enough power to escape? He needed to get back. He rose from the building and followed the silvery thread of power back to his body.

Shenella woke up early. Grabbing the cloth she had placed carefully over the subdued glass bowl beside the bed, she pulled it gently towards her. A mellow purple light emanated through the room. This was so strange but yet so familiar. She must have been underwater before. How else she could explain how calm she was?

Someone had thoughtfully placed a set of clothes made of sea grass at the end of the bed while she slept. Picking them up she saw they were blue trousers and a small blue top similar to those she had seen the day before. As if she didn't feel and look foreign enough she was now dressed in a different color to everyone else.

She had just finished tying her hair back when Sori walked in. *'Are you ready for breakfast?'*

'I feel like I'm ready for anything. What do you eat?' She laughed nervously.

'We're vegetarians. Don't worry, we don't eat fish!'

Getting up from the bed edge she followed him outside. As she stepped past the door she started sinking rapidly. She suddenly remembered they were at the top of a canyon! They were in the sea of course they didn't need streets. Kicking her legs she stabilized. Sori, laughing at her swam down to join her.

'You forgot where we were didn't you! Come

on, let's go and eat.'

He swam slowly so she could keep up, but she was still tired by the time they arrived at a large hall. She'd forgotten to use the crystal.

Although it looked the same as the rest, the room had a series of rounded doors and windows visible from the outside; this one did not have any curtains. Men and women sat on long low tables on the lower floor while stairs led up to a long gallery where the food was laid out. Sori took her upstairs and helped her choose.

Shenella felt awkward swimming with a bowl of food but she followed Sori's lead and held the bowl with her hand covering the opening so the vegetation wouldn't fall out. He led her to the corner and they sat by a window that overlooked the canyon. Outside the same mixture of greens and yellows from the climbing plants still glowed and every now and then people swam past, some in couples, some in small groups.

What now? She thought. She couldn't go back; Aras would kill her. Even if he hadn't found out that she was Elementi royalty, he would still kill her for running away. Despair filled her. Sori saw her distress and put his arm around her.

'It'll be all right, Shenella.'

At the main doors there was a stir as the reception committee she saw last night came in. They were dressed differently from the previous evening, wearing more colors. When they saw Sori and Shenella, they made their way straight to their table.

Their grim faces were the first things that Shenella noticed when they sat down. Sitting up straighter in response she waited to hear what they had to say.

'We've just had word back. Aras is furious. It's official; he's declared war on us. But if what Sori said is true,' the Kinar looked Shenella in the eyes, *'the High-King may be coming back. Aras has taken to his bed. The priests think his renewed illness means the High-King has arrived on Eleria. However, even with just the High-King and the Water Queen, it may still be possible to unseat Aras and send the Magi back to the Dark Continent. Will you help us?'*

Shenella paused, fork halfway to her lips. Of course she would help. There wasn't much else she could do. Her whole life was built on a lie. She needed to get revenge for the death of her parents. She couldn't remember her real parents clearly, but she recalled the love and the agony of her father's death and her foster parents' 'accident' was still fresh in her mind, even after two years.

Her decision shone in her eyes. *'Yes!'*

Chero looked relieved. *'You will want to go to the temple. I'm not sure if your parents will have taken you there before, but you will need it to contact the High-King. If he is here you will be able to talk to him. Finish your meal and Sori will take you. He is your high priest as well as your ambassador.'* Shenella twisted to look at Sori. He grinned shamefaced.

'Didn't I tell you?'

Slotting back into his body, Jake came to with Kiera and Mirim looking down at him concerned.

"I couldn't find him," he said. "The trail went cold - I'm exhausted." Jake pushed himself up and stretched, "How long was I gone?"

"Only about an hour, I've brought some maps in from another room. We can combine our minds and do a search using it - if you are feeling up to it?"

"Mirim, no offence but I need a break. It's night, I'm tired, you're tired and I can see that Kiera is tired too. There must be some bedrooms around here; it used to house a complete city!"

Mirim shrugged. "All right."

She put the maps down and carefully placed them on a shelf next to the door.

"Follow me."

The main control room led off to several apartments. The first five were the largest. A couple of the other doors were open and he could see they were smaller and empty. They must have either converted it from several apartments to make them bigger or made smaller he thought. Either way it wasn't a coincidence there was one for each of the five Royal Houses.

Jake peered into Kiera's room before she closed the door. It seemed they liked to color code. Hers was green as his had rich cream and white fabrics.

"You'd think the family would use the opportunity to use other colors" he joked to Karl as they entered the High-King's apartment.

"They probably needed the color schemes to tell them apart." He replied opening a cupboard door. "Where am I going to sleep?"

Mirim stood behind them, "I wasn't expecting anyone else, but there is another room which the servants used behind there." She pointed to a door Jake and Karl had missed in their quick inspection. Karl waited before the door closed.

"Charming. Bossy isn't she?"

"Yeah, probably not used to people." Jake thought about the loneliness he felt during their merge.

"Did you just hear her, she probably thinks of me as a bleeding servant."

"Ignore her."

"Easy for you to say, you're one of them. Clearly I can't look after myself. My sword fighting is better than yours, and I did go to Judo for two weeks."

Jake and Karl looked at each other for a moment before Jake raised an eyebrow at the thought. There was a second of quiet before they both burst into laughter.

"Imagine getting her in an arm lock." gulped Karl.

"I think that's wrestling," snorted Jake, "but she could probably do with it."

CHAPTER FOURTEEN - WATER QUEEN

Adramelech hung in no-space, consumed by thoughts. The boy must have felt the fire element. To get to him all he had to do was to appear somewhere and his natural form would do the rest. There was only one problem with this plan. The boy would be wondering why he couldn't track him before.

He would have to appear by a volcano he decided. Ironic, after setting one off on Earth, he was going to use the same one on Eleria. That was what was so great about interdimensional travel he mused. If you knew roughly where something was in one world there was a high percentage chance it would be there in most of the dimensions.

Actually no, he changed his mind. He would

need a more active volcano than that one and there was only one active volcano in this part of the world. Decision made, he returned to normal space and time.

The next morning Jake woke up to Mirim banging on the door. *That girl is keen,* he thought.

"Okay, Okay!"

Picking up his clothes from the floor he dressed quickly and rushed to the control room. "What's the rush?"

Kiera walked in from another door sleepy-eyed.

"I used the crystals to scout the city, and they know you are here. Your presence in Eleria is making Aras even more ill. They know where we are! They're preparing their army!" Mirim burst out in a rush.

Kiera looked confused, "Slow down, slow down. How did you get to Eleria?"

Mirim sat down heavily on the chair by her console. "We're in Eleria. The capital is called Naven. I went there the same way Jake did last night. I astral projected. I was listening to one of his advisers, and I don't know how but he knew I was there! I came back as soon as I realized but I found out that Aras followed you back last night. He's able to leave his body too.

It is the only way he can cope with the pain. He must have sensed you and followed you back."

Mirim's voice rose, "No one has known where the Citadel is for thousands of years, apart from the five families. You're back for one night and the Magi know exactly where it is. Do you know what they could do with the power in this place?"

Jake shrugged, "So he knows exactly where we are. We're underwater, right?" She nodded. "So how are they going to get to us?"

She rolled her eyes. "He may only be half an Elementi but his other half is Magi. They have the power of illusion and what they can't do through illusion they have their armies and creatures they trap from other dimensions."

"Eh, you never mentioned that before."

"They can't travel between dimensions. Oh sure, they did once - that's how they came to this world. Sometime in the past they lost that ability. They can still reach out and trap aliens though. If a being is already moving through the dimensions, if they are in no-space, they are fair game to them.

"They don't understand how it works any more but they know enough to build barriers. I saw one of their lesser mages on Pumar once. It was amazing. He obviously wasn't that good or he wouldn't have been entertaining guests at the island, but he was still worth watching. He created whole views in front of us. One moment we were on the island and the next I could have sworn I was transported physically to Naven. He ended his act with the trapping of a Deoc."

"What's a Deoc?" Kiera interrupted.

"A creature made of fire. In the dimensions everything has a possibility," she explained. "There are beings made of pure fire, or water, or air or even earth. That's how my ancestors and your parents got you out. Since these beings are pure energy they are able to travel through the dimensions a lot easier than we ever could. The Elementi used them as guardians for their children for centuries. When the children were old enough to look after themselves the beings return to where they come from. Unlike with the Magi though, these creatures served us willingly. There was genuine respect between us, before the change there were regular cultural exchanges.

"The ones who helped you would have probably died on Earth. There are some places that are anathema to them, where they can't survive. We are not sure why but Earth is one of those places. They were brave to take you. I hope they escaped in time."

Annoyed at the side-track, Kiera tried to bring the conversation back round to the danger. "How long do we have before the Emperor's army gets here?" she demanded.

"Two days minimum, four days at the most," Mirim replied quietly.

"Well I vote we go back to Earth," Jake said. "He can't follow us there - you said so yourself." Turning to Kiera he asked, "What about you? This isn't our fight. This was our parent's life - not ours. We still have a choice."

"I think we should stay. What have we got to look forward to at home? I don't have a life there, and what will yours be like? Here you are... you will be the next High-King! At home you would probably spend a couple more years at school, three at University and a dead-end job working in computers or maybe banking. Wouldn't you rather be royalty?"

"We could get killed here!"

"I told you that you can't go back, not for months anyway. If it's any consolation, he won't destroy this place. He will want to be able to use the Matrix and he can't do that except from in here. All the gates were disabled at the time of the Change, so he will only be able to get through by teleporting - he won't have enough power for that. He could only get here by using the pathway from the island. Once they get here, it won't be long before they discover that."

"So, what are our choices," he demanded.

"We need to unite the Elementi here. They won't be a match for us reunited. They were only able to defeat our ancestors before because of trickery. That won't happen again."

"Okay, where's that map." Resigned he held his hand out.

Ignoring his hand, Mirim pulled up a table he hadn't noticed before and spread out a map of the planet.

"Big enough is it?" Jake asked sarcastically. He was beginning to like the older girl less and less. He was still furious.

Mirim replied. "We don't need a detailed map; it's only a starting point for us. It anchors us to reality."

"Why can't we project a map on the wall?"

"We could, but it works better to have something solid under your hands."

Crystals at the ready, all three joined their minds together. Karl looked on from the doorway and brushed his hair back with his fingers. He subconsciously wiped the gel on his trousers. There wasn't anything he could help with. He moved off into the corridor. If they were going to be there a while, he may as well do something useful. There might be some clothes around or, and he brightened at the thought, there might be some cool gadgets! He took another look at his friend and decided to go exploring.

Jake connected to the Matrix first, bringing along the other two, first Kiera, Mirim. He found it easier to connect to Kiera than Mirim, maybe because Mirim had grown up in an alien world to him.

It felt natural to become part of the Matrix, he was whole again. As he stared at the map, it shimmered before his eyes to become the world as if from a bird's-eye view. It looked much like his own world he thought. Their minds swept west over the ocean until they reached a large land mass.

'That's America,' he thought. Mirim's thought reached him, 'We call it the Dark Continent. It's where the Magi live. They appeared about three hundred years ago. Our people ignored them at first but they soon got our attention after their killing spree.' Her thoughts filled with bitterness.

Their minds floated over the world, searching systematically. He must be somewhere! He could feel the others' despair when they passed through what he knew as Asia with no sign of the rogue element. Continuing west they soon arrived back at Europe. He was about to give up when he felt... something? It was just a twinge but it was enough to get his attention.

Halting in mid-air he oriented himself - he was over Italy. He recognized the shape. Heart in his mouth, he descended. *No it couldn't be. That's just too weird.* He'd visited there when he was ten. Pompeii, but it wasn't how he remembered it. He tried to reconcile what he could see with what he remembered. There was the volcano but the towns weren't there. Only one small village existed at the foot of the volcano.

Kiera was the first to notice it was smoking. *'He has to be here,'* she shared her thought with the other two. *'Go down and have a look.'*

'No,' that thought he saw came from Mirim. *'We know he will be here. We'll never find him out here with just our astral selves; he is next to the most powerful source of his element there is. It will mask him easily. He may not be planning to hide, but he will be hidden next to that volcano.'*

Mirim dropped out of the connection taking Kiera too. Reluctantly Jake let the familiar meld go to find he was staring at the map with a cross marked neatly over Italy.

"We need to go to Italy," he said.

"Somara" Mirim corrected, "We are not on Earth anymore."

The temple wasn't what Shenella expected. Only a short swim away, it looked like it had been raised from the seabed. The walls were covered in coral and unlike the canyon there were no glowing plants over it.

Sori beside her, sensing her question answered it unasked.

'This temple is hidden. It would not do to advertise its presence. Only a few of us know exactly where it is. All the Merpeople are unquestionably loyal of course, there would be no point in betraying the people. We couldn't live with the humans for too long. Many of our people have no interest in the temple, partly so if anyone were captured they wouldn't be able to betray its location but partly because they know it is looked after. They don't have to believe in the Water Queen or Goddess. They know she exists!

'The temple is powered by the tides. I am no engineer and couldn't tell you how it works - only that it does. It is pretty though isn't it?'

Shenella agreed. The reds, pinks and yellows of the coral were an arresting sight. Shenella and Sori hung in the water meters away from the building using only the light they carried to see it.

'*Once we are inside,*' Sori continued, '*it won't be so dark. There are lights there like magic, though I know they are not. You place your hand on them and the walls just light up. It is miraculous. So much was lost during the Magi reign!*'

At the entrance there was a small bare room. They floated in gently. Sori covered his lamp and pulled a lever on the wall. The door closed and a long slow hiss told him the water was being drawn away from the room. Within seconds the room was free of water, replaced with clean smelling air.

"Ready?" he asked.

Astounded and very wet, she realized, she followed him as he entered the next room. It was another small bare room. She was about to question Sori again when a warm breeze came from the corners to dry them. When they were dry, Sori stepped forward to press another lever.

They emerged into a room she guessed was twice the size of the great hall in the castle in

Naven. She guessed they were in the middle of the building, in the foyer. On the floor was the Aquel crest, a fountain carved into the rock. Looking up she could see four, no five stories. The walls were a brilliant white and each level had a balcony.

"Is that - Salarian stone?" She was impressed.

"Yes"

"How did they get it down here?"

"Who knows? The Elementi did it centuries ago. This way."

His steps echoed on the stone floor. Climbing the stairs he stared behind at her with a raised brow, "Are you coming?"

"Um yes, sorry." She hurried to climb the stairs after him. *The Merpeople were minimalist,* she thought. There was no decoration at all that she could see. Corridor after corridor was a featureless white. No pictures, just white floor and white walls. *It was all very different from the castle,* she thought. The old Elementi place was filled with pictures of the current and old royal families. *They wouldn't want anyone to question the unbroken hereditary line of the Emperor now would they?*

Right at the top of the building, they arrived, out of breath, at a room that covered the entire floor. Shenella stared in wonder at the ceiling.

She could see the sea though it. Without thought she reached up on her tiptoes to touch it. Her fingertips met a tingling barrier - not the glass she was expecting.

Sori enjoying her surprise gently moved her aside to walk past her to get to the pedestal in the middle. It was made of the same stone as the walls and floor. She moved closer, curious.

At the top of the pedestal was a carved hand. It looked like it should be holding something. Instinctively, she took out her crystal from the pouch she'd found in the underwater apartment that now hung around her waist. Sori nodded in encouragement. She studied it for a moment and slotted the stone into the hand and stepped back. Bright light flashed from the crystal illuminating the room.

When the light faded, she looked around in confusion. Sori still stood beside her but the room no longer looked bare. Sensing his thoughts she knew Sori couldn't see what she could. She extended her awareness around him so he could share it.

There was a semi-circular table in front of her. It had five types of colored crystals embedded in it. Red, yellow, white, green and... With her enhanced dual perception, she could see the ghostly image of the pedestal superimposed on the blue section.

There were three other people in the room she counted. They hadn't noticed her yet, which gave her the opportunity to study them. They were all young, the boy she judged to be around fourteen with bright straw-colored hair. He could almost be Aras' younger brother she thought. The other two were probably slightly older than her, maybe fifteen or sixteen years old, she guessed.

The girl in yellow held herself more confidently than the other two she noticed. They were all strangely dressed. The yellow garments were old-fashioned but the outfits from the other two were unfamiliar.

The trio bent over a map. Sori gasped beside her. Through their connection Shenella heard the thought he sent her, "The Elementi are almost complete. Look at the consoles, the only color not fully lit up is red!"

Kiera noticed her first. Mirim and Jake were sniping at each other again. She was tactfully trying to avoid getting involved, looking at the consoles she was surprised to see the blue one lit up in front of her. Out of the corner of her eye she saw movement. Turning slowly, she was confronted by the sight of a younger girl. She was blond with piercing sea-green eyes.

Behind her was a second ghostly figure of a man. Kiera reached behind her and tapped Jake's arm. He didn't respond. She tapped him again.

"Kiera, hang on a minute." he said not turning around. She tapped him again, this time more insistently.

"Jake!"

He spun around. "What? Oh."

Mirim in mid-flow followed his gaze. She took in the girl's appearance, noting the sea grass material of her outfit.

"Shey!" she exclaimed.

"How did you get in?" Jake demanded.

Mirim put a soothing hand on his arm.

"It's all right; she's not here. She must be broadcasting from the temple?" She waited for Shenella's confirmation. Getting a nod, she continued.

"All our families had ways of accessing the Matrix from their strongholds but most of them were destroyed by the Magi or just fell into disrepair. The Merpeople must have been looking after theirs. I suppose it helps the satellite station for the water element was also their temple."

Jake took charge, "Hi. My name is Jake, this is

Kiera and this is Mirim. What's yours?"

"My name is Shenella. I am in a temple near the Merpeople city. I should warn you, Aras knows you exist. He doesn't know about all of you though," she stared pointedly at Mirim and Kiera. "we think he only knows about me and... Jake isn't it?"

Mirim cut in. "We have found the Fire King's location. We've got two days to find him and get him back from Somara."

"There's an active volcano there," the younger girl frowned.

"Don't worry; we don't need you for that. You are far more use to us where you are. Your power is strongest there, you may not know it but you are not too far away in distance either. All you have to do is stay in that room and we can keep in contact with you easily."

"All right." Shenella reached forward and took the crystal from the plinth. The other room disappeared and she was alone again with Sori.

"Did you see that?"

"...And heard it. Thank you for allowing me to join you. You'll need to practice your powers, if we are to be of help to the others. It's going to be a long day."

CHAPTER FIFTEEN - DANI

"...I thought we didn't have enough power to teleport?" Jake said.

"What I said was, there wasn't enough power to send you back to Earth. Besides we are not teleporting." Mirim explained patiently, "We are using a Gate."

"Didn't you say the gates were all destroyed earlier?" Kiera asked.

Mirim slung a light canvas bag over her shoulder and rounded on the two. "Why are you two questioning everything I say?"

"We're not. It's just you lied about getting back and you aren't making any sense. One minute we can't teleport the next we are but aren't. The Gates are destroyed and a moment later they are not. You're confusing us!" Jake was exasperated. "What are we supposed to think? We don't know you from Adam."

"Who...?"

"Doesn't matter, we don't know you but we are supposed to just trust you like that." He snapped his finger.

"I could say the same thing about you." Mirim retorted.

"Difference is - you came to find us, not the other way around!"

Kiera moved between them. "OK, you two - calm down. We have to be here and our lives are in danger unless we can find this other person. We need to work together. Let's just agree to trust each other." She looked from one to the other, "Agreed?"

"Agreed," they mumbled.

Kiera picked up the map of Somara.

"Do we need this?" Taking Mirim's nod as assent, she rolled it up and gave it to her. "Okay, lead on to the gate."

Grudgingly Mirim moved off. The gates were on the lower levels. Even though they had been disabled, Mirim had been taught by her mother how to repair them in case she needed them in the future. As they trudged down the stairs, Mirim explained they were easy to disable again, you just asked the Matrix to do it.

It was only unusable for those without the power. If Aras tried, he probably could - it just wouldn't occur to him. Before stepping though Mirim saw to it that only those with crystals could pass through. That way if they were chased she explained to the others, they wouldn't be able to follow them into the Citadel.

Mirim walked through the portal first. Kiera shrugged at Jake and followed. Before he could dwell too long on what he was doing he took a deep breath, stepped back and made a running jump through. He expected to feel... something. There was nothing except Kiera's arm as he narrowly missed crashing into the girl. Veering to the side he stumbled on a jagged rock. Sharp pain travelled up his foot before he righted himself. He stood up and the heat hit him. Of course, he thought, Italy would be a lot warmer than the heat regulated Citadel. Mirim stood back and looked at him quizzically.

Jake took off his black hoodie and tied it around his waist looking anywhere but at Mirim. *This was ridiculous,* he chided himself. He raised his eyes and glared at Mirim asking, "So where do we go from here?" He looked around, they were in a cave and the temperature was stifling but the breeze coming from the cave mouth just made it bearable.

Kiera sensing their moods rounded on them.

"What is wrong with you two? You've done nothing but snipe at each other for hours!" They both looked away unable to look her in the eyes.

"Jake, you need to get over that you can't go home yet. You may even get to like it here if we live long enough. Mirim may be bossy but it's because she's been on her own for so long." Mirim's head jerked up.

"Yes, Mirim. You need to learn that you can't be the leader all the time. Jake will have to lead us some of the time just because he is who he is. He may be younger and he does need to grow up, but you need to treat him with a bit more respect. Do you two understand?"

Jake held his hand to Mirim, "I'm sorry. I forget that you were on your own for such a long time."

"It's all right. I'll try not to patronize. And I forget that you didn't grow up here, that you are hearing most of this for the first time."

"Ok, now that you've both kissed and made up, we need to find that boy!" Kiera stalked out of the cave.

"She's a bit annoyed." Jake said. "Well, we

may as well follow." They trailed behind.

The sunlight was bright after being inside for so long. It took a few seconds to adjust but the view was amazing.

"I wish I'd brought my surfboard." Jake joked. Kiera smiled.

Mirim looked at the other two not understanding and huffed. She began to walk in the direction of the sun.

"The volcano is due east. We are going to the village of Somara, which lies at the bottom. The volcano erupted centuries ago and the Elementi tried to move the people on because of the danger but they refused. There is one consolation - this is so remote we are unlikely to meet any Empire militia... and..." She grinned, forgetting her earlier annoyance. "The journey will all be flat!"

It took an hour to reach the village. Once they had travelled past some trees blocking their view they could see the volcano easily. As they drew nearer Jake felt as if the last element was calling him. This was the last missing piece of the puzzle.

At times the ground was thick with underbrush. It was a struggle to step over the harsh, thorny branches. At others the smell of wild fruit trees exhilarated them and made them happy to be outside in the sun.

As they neared the village they saw it was small. There was one street leading away from the volcano with several houses, a blacksmith, inn and a small shop. Passing the blacksmith, Jake felt a frisson or fear. He halted suddenly. Kiera, seconds behind, bumped into him.

"Here?" she asked.

He nodded, "Somewhere here."

"It has to be the blacksmith, come on."

Jake led the way and they headed for the smithy. An old building, like the rest of the street, it was made from large grey stones. A sculpted sign in the shape of a hammer striking an anvil proclaimed the building's purpose. Inside it was dark, the only light coming from a fire in the wall but they could make out a large burly man holding a long pole hammering its end on the anvil. He swung it over to a vat of water and it hissed as it hit the cool water.

Behind him, Mirim saw the shadow of someone else. She could feel the energy that radiated off him. He had to be the one. The man came forward to them at the entrance, and he addressed Jake. "Can I help you?"

"Hello. You don't know us, but we need to talk."

The figure studied them for a moment before

calling to the older man, "I won't be long." The Smith didn't hear and carried on hammering the anvil with great strokes. The man in the shadows pointed to the door and followed them out into the light.

They emerged outside and blinked in the brightness.

"We need your help. We are trying to unite the last of the five Elementi families. We believe you are the last of the Firelli family - the fire element." Jake stopped, something wasn't right. He could feel the rage simmering in the other man. There wasn't any reason for him to be angry.

"Does this sound familiar to you in any way?" Jake asked, his voice rose slightly.

"I've been waiting a long time for this. I was told I was the new Fire King when my father died. I was told to keep hidden." The man furtively glanced down either side of the street. Seeing no one, he clicked his fingers on his right hand. A small flame shot out of his thumb.

"Well there's no doubt there " Kiera said. "Let's go."

Dani was bored. There hadn't been a single customer all day. That was always the problem with market week; all the wine growers went to the city. That wouldn't be so bad but they also took their wives and families with them too. Business would be slow for another week after that as they went through the supplies they brought back from the city. He didn't know why Fis didn't just close the shop for two weeks and take a holiday himself. No. Scratch that - let them both take a holiday. They'd be lucky if one person came in each week.

He sighed. There was just nothing to do. He'd tidied the shelves, cleaned the counters and swept the floor. There had to be more to life than this. Picking up the broom again he decided to sweep the porch outside. If Fis came to check up on him at least the place would be spotless.

Opening the door quietly - the bell jarred on his nerves - he saw a group of people standing across the street outside the blacksmith. They were trying to be quiet but their voices carried over to him easily. He was about to ignore them when he caught a fragment of their conversation.

"I've been waiting a long time for this. I was told I was the new Fire King when my father died."

What? Who were these people? That man

was no Fire King. The group evidently thought he was because they started walking off with him. Dani let them go, he'd better talk to Brigid and quickly.

Taking out his key he locked the door behind him and started to run towards the volcano. When he was sure he was out of earshot of the village, he slowed down. The sandy surface was slippery underneath his feet. When he judged himself halfway up he started calling for his guardian. "Brigid! Brigid!"

Facing the volcano he saw the air shimmer as she materialized. The flames died as she covered her form with skin and clothing. The familiar middle-aged appearance of his guardian stood before him.

"What's wrong?"

"There were some strangers in the village." He said breathless. "I heard one of them say to the others he was the Fire King and they just left. Isn't it a bit of a coincidence they would show up here?"

"No, it's the only active volcano around here, but why come and go...?" Her eyes looked into the distance - a faraway expression stole across her face. "I can see them now; there were two boys and two girls?"

"Yes, the man who said he was the Fire King

was older than the others. I've never seen him before."

"All right. I will have a look."

Brigid covered her face with her hands as she concentrated. Within moments she began to shudder. Her hands flew away from her face as she contorted with fear. Dani rushed forward to catch her as she collapsed. Sitting her down on the ground he asked, "Are you all right?"

"He's not human," she gasped. "I would recognize him anywhere. That's Adramelech. The other boy, I took a good look before I saw Adramelech. He may be the High-King. He has a touch of the fire element in him.

"You will have to stop them before they take him wherever they are going. It may well be to the Citadel I told you about. He will want to take over the Matrix, if he does, this and other worlds could be destroyed at his whim."

She leant against Dani while he helped her stand up.

"I'm getting old, Dani. I have watched over your family for over a hundred years. I was a young girl when I arrived and it is near my time to leave. I may as well go with a bang." She ruffled his red hair. "I've known you your entire life, and it's time we came out of hiding. First I must give you something."

She held out her hand. A small red box appeared. He grasped it and felt the cool metal under his fingers. Something in it called to him. He knew if he opened the box his simple life would change.

It opened with surprising ease despite its advanced age. Inside was a small red crystal. In wonder he picked it up and cradled it in his hands. Immediately, the world exploded in fire around him. The sheer power of the volcano beneath him called him to use it. He was aware of everything that contained heat - the sun, the earth and even the being before him. For the first time in his life he understood her. He could feel her vast age. He was saddened; her life was cut shorter to be with him. She had kept the volcano dormant for so long that her life-force had depleted. Upon closer look, her realized that she wasn't old at all. Her energy had simply drained away with the sustained effort of holding the volcano's destructive force at bay.

Dani looked up at the sky. The sun was the only energy source which could help her now. He felt the sun's heat on his skin and called for more. He began to absorb it, retaining the pure energy. The crystal glowed a deep red in his hand just as he began to shine from the absorbed sunlight. Facing Brigid he held out his hand. She took it understanding what he planned to do. The energy jumped to her like a bolt of lightning. There was a loud crack and she flailed back with the force, collapsing again on the ground, her face covered by her arm.

Fearing the worst, he ran to her. Relieved, he could still see her breathing. He drew her arm carefully away. The face staring back at him looked thirty years younger in human terms. Using his other senses, he checked her energy levels. Sighing with relief he gently called her name.

She smiled back up at him. She had always chosen long hair in the forms she chose but now it was a luscious red not unlike his own, though her familiar eyes still marked her as alien with their red tinge. He began to help her up but she refused the assistance. To his horror, as he watched, wrinkles began to snake across her face again, her hair became duller and her eyes dimmer. The changes reversed until the old familiar face stood before him.

"I'm so sorry." Dani murmured, touching his friend's cheek.

"It's too late, I am too old and I must return home. They must be heading to the gate. There is one about an hour's walk away. You need to get there first, you will have to run."

"What about you?"

"I will be all right. Your destiny is not with me. I will only slow you down. The gates are in the caves by the trees. Go!"

Dani began to run. His long legs pumped as he negotiated the sand and the underbrush. Within minutes he reached the tree line, but there was no sign of the others. His lungs burned with the effort. He stopped and scanned the beach. Caves, what caves? He saw a flash of yellow as he saw the strangers move into the darkness of a hidden cave. He began to run again. He had to get there before they left!

The entrance to the cave was small but the ceiling was just above his head height so he didn't have to crouch. The gate was beyond the pillars in front of him. The four symbols engraved on them, water and fire on one, earth and air on the other, glowed with intensity. He tried to shout but he was too late. Adramelech was the last to go through, holding on to the back of Jake's hoodie. He saw Dani and gave him a sly grin before disappearing through. Dani dived for the gate, desperate to grab the pretender. As he reached the gate the lights dimmed and it shut down. Dani hit his fist on the hard stone. He was too late!

Adramelech's looked around with glee as he dropped the material from the boy's clothing. He was here. Finally here! Still, he looked at the humans beside him with caution. It would not do to underestimate them. They could still defeat him if they worked together. There must be a way of separating them.

So this was the famous Citadel. He looked out of the tower window at the fish swimming by and shivered. There was too much water here for his liking.

Jake strode in, hands deep within his pockets when he noticed Adramelech's shiver.

"Are you OK?"

"Fine. I was just thinking about all the water."

"Yeah, it is a bit creepy, but it does protect us. I suppose being the fire element it must really freak you out."

Adramelech agreed with the young human.

"Is it just you three here?" Adramelech casually asked.

"No, my friend Karl is here too. I was just going to go looking for him but I think he's gone exploring. This place is huge. It's probably safer for him to be out of the way anyway."

"Does he have any power?"

"No, he's just a friend from back home." Jake laughed. "He followed us when we teleported here."

"Mirim has lived here her whole life, and she will show you your rooms. It's getting late." Kiera interjected as they climbed the stairs.

"I was hoping I wasn't going to stay here too long."

"I know how you feel. I was only coming here for the day." Jake chuckled. "Anyway, I'm going to look for Karl for a while then I'm going to sleep. I figure he can look after himself though."

CHAPTER SIXTEEN - PRISON

The next morning Kiera burst into Jake's room, Adramelech followed closely behind.

"Mirim's gone!"

"Wha-a-"

"Mirim's gone. She went to the castle again, but she never came back. It's been an hour. She said she was only going to be gone a couple of minutes!"

"Mirim can look after herself." Jake groaned and pulled the covers over his head.

"Jake, she's been gone an hour!"

"All right, Ok, I'm coming. That girl is nothing but trouble."

Moments later, Jake was up and connected to the Matrix. The crystal mind greeted him, becoming more intelligent as the seconds passed. Its thoughts joined with Jake's as they swirled in crystal vortex. It would be easy to lose himself he realized. He thought of Mirim and the Matrix thoughts rippled with color as it recognized the image.

"Send me to Mirim." asked Jake.

The room changed instantly. Jake looked around in confusion. This wasn't what he was expecting. It didn't look right. His mind tried to connect to the white cord of power and the Matrix. It wasn't there! He whirled around. He was in his body! How, huh?

Mirim was sitting on a low stool, the only other object in the white room staring at him.

"Hello Jake."

"Where are we?" he asked.

"I don't know. I went to Naven to see what was happening with Aras and suddenly found myself here."

Jake paused, looking around the featureless room. There were no windows, just two doors, one in front and one to his right.

"What's with everything being white here? And have you even tried the doors?"

Mirim only glared at him. Did he think she was an idiot?

"Be my guest."

Jake shrugged. Mirim had been here for an hour. Why was she just sitting there? Why wasn't she trying to escape? Aras knew the location of the Citadel, Kiera, Karl and Adra would not be safe. They couldn't possibly hold the stronghold with only two powers against Magi magic.

He strode to the door and paused for a moment before opening it. He looked back at Mirim, but she just challenged him with that same glare. Fine, if that was how she wanted to play it!

He yanked the door open. A pale yellow mist billowed out from the frame. He coughed before it settled into a dense cloud inside the doorframe. He looked at Mirim. He tentatively moved his hand through the mist and brought it sharply back. His hand was still there. He stood taller and puffed his chest out. They had to get out of here! Taking a small gulp of air, he went back a couple of steps and held his breath as he ran forward through the door.

He expected to feel a twinge as he passed through the air but felt nothing. He let his breath go in disappointment. The room was the same. The same two doors, although on different walls. Mirim stepped into the room behind him.

"Tried the door, Jake?" She raised one ironic eyebrow.

Jake scowled, "How many rooms have you been in?"

"About twenty. I only stopped at the last one because it had a stool. There wasn't any furniture in the other rooms I tried."

"Where are we?"

"I think we're in the Matrix."

"Why?"

"The yellow mist. It's like the air power. No one but the Matrix or an air power could create that."

Jake's eyebrows knitted together as he thought this through.

"Why would the Matrix trap us here?"

"Maybe it thought it was doing us a favor? I was in Aras' castle, and you followed me. We must have been in danger."

"O-k-a-y, but why wouldn't the Matrix communicate with us?"

Mirim went quiet for a moment before continuing, "Maybe it can't because we are in its mind rather than being part of it."

"Woah. Hang on a minute. You are telling me the Matrix thought we were in danger and so yanked us out of Aras" castle and teleported us with our bodies to inside its mind?'

"Do you have a better theory?"

Jake snorted. "My gerbil would have a better theory than that!"

"Since you're so intelligent, you find a way out!" She stormed back through the door they'd come through.

Jake started after her and shrugged again. What was with this girl? She may be older but she always gave up far too easy. He took a step forward to join her but changed his mind. It made more sense to explore this place. Mirim wasn't going to find a way out - it was up to him.

Meanwhile in the Citadel, Adramelech stood alone in the main control room. Kiera had gone to look at the hydroponics level and would be gone for at least an hour more. He could barely hold in his glee. *This was it! This was all that I have been working for.* The power of his natural form was nothing compared to the power he could wield with the Citadel.

He almost laughed as he considered how easy it was to trick those idiot children into thinking he was one of them. Just one measly flame and they believed he was the Fire King. Idiots. As he walked to the crystals that made fire, the floor jerked. Adramelech righted himself but was thrown off balance by another jerk. His head turned towards one of the windows. The Citadel was rising!

No matter, with single-minded determination, Adramelech moved forward to reach the console. With a triumphal roar he touched the red crystals. The power would be his! He grasped the biggest crystals, expecting a rush of energy. He paused. There was nothing. Confused he stared down at them. Tentatively he pushed some of his power on to the crystal - it glowed for a second absorbing the power but still nothing. He moved closer and pushed more power through. The crystals glowed again for a moment more but still no reciprocal power answered his call.

The truth flashed in his mind. You had to be human to connect. His frustration grew. It was not enough to possess an element, there had to be the combination. Of course, that was why the Magi could not use this power. He glared at the crystals, and his eyes glowed red with anger.

Adramelech heard a sound behind him and turned, Kiera was standing by the door staring at him.

"What are you doing? Did you feel tha-a-?"

her voice trailed off as she saw Adramelech's face. His grasp of his human form began to fail as he became angrier. Flames licked his face as his hair became fire. Where his eyes once were, red pits of flame lingered. Kiera screamed.

Jake was getting worried. He'd walked through about ten rooms now and he was getting nowhere. At the eleventh room, he found Mirim again, sat on the same small stool.

"Are you OK?" Her voice was softer than before. She got up to draw closer to him. She'd made her point but Jake wasn't ready yet to give in. She put her hand on his arm and a jolt of electricity arced between them. They both jumped back in surprise.

"What was that?" Jake exclaimed.

"We're getting stronger." Mirim's hazel eyes were sad. "If we can't get out it won't help us."

"We can't give up. There has to be a way out. We have to at least try." Jake grabbed Mirim's hands. "Come on."

She nodded and let him lead her to the next room.

"Is that it?" Aras asked as he entered Ecu's laboratory.

"Yes, Sire." Ecu held up the large white crystal in the palm of his hand. "This prison has hundreds of refracted rooms. They won't even know they are in a prison. They could walk around for years and never get out. With no food or water their bodies will wither in a week."

Aras nodded. It was a fitting death. He looked down at his own emaciated form. The living death he had been suffering for weeks would now be Malo's fate. He grinned. He was feeling better already. Whatever power the boy was using was trapped within the prison and would not be able to affect him. Without two powers the Citadel was easy pickings.

Adramelech grunted and dove for Kiera. He flew across the control room with one bound. As he jumped he lost all semblance of humanity in a burst of fire. He caught her, careful not to burn his prize, and dragged her to the control room. If he couldn't use the crystals he could control someone who could!

"STOP!"

Adramelech twisted at the sound of the voice and growled. The vivid reds of the flames turned blue as he recognized the speaker. Dani stood before him, one of the villagers from beside the volcano. Adramelech reached out and met the answering tinge of the fire element. So this was the Fire King. Oh, but he was weak.

"I said stop."

"What do you want, human?"

"Leave her alone! It's me you want. I am the Fire King."

Adramelech paused and turned again to look at the interloper. Instinctively he scanned the human's body and laughed. This was the Fire King? The red tell-tale thread of power was clear to see - but it was no match for a Deoc.

"Leave while you still can. What are you going to do about it, little human?"

Dani moved forward and held out his hand with the red crystal prominent. "I will defeat you, foul demon."

Adramelech laughed.

"Can't you come up with anything more original than that?" Adramelech sneered. He almost felt sorry the boy would die too quickly.

In the crystal prison, Jake entered another room, this time the mist was red and he frowned. The mist was different in each doorway but four colors of the elements had been there, white was missing. His mind mulled this over as he went from room to room. The electric shocks from Mirim jarring him as they accidentally brushed past each other.

"We're not in the Matrix," he suddenly said.

"We have to be."

"What color has been missing?"

Mirim's gaze turned thoughtful.

"White? There is no white mist."

"This isn't the Matrix. Instead, it's like the colors have separated like a prism. This has to be some sort of prison... and if it is a crystal we should be able to get out of it. After all, we get our powers from crystal."

"How?"

"The electric shocks." He thought aloud. "We can combine our powers and get out." He turned his excited face to hers. "Take my hand."

They joined hands and felt their energy moving from one to the other building in intensity. Sparks began to fly off them. Mirim let go.

"You have to trust me, Mirim."

Mirim looked at the younger boy. Why couldn't she trust him? She was annoyed at him, yes, but that didn't explain it. She analyzed her feelings. She didn't like being told what to do. That was it. No one had told her what to do before, at least not since her mother died but here was the next High-King. No, he *was* the High-King, he deserved her fealty and trust.

Jake saw the conflicted feelings flit across her face. He tentatively took hold of her hand again. She let him. The air temperature became warm, cold, and finally very hot. The energy was painful as it coursed between them. Mirim cried out. Jake shouted for her to hold on. The sound of broken glass surrounded them and they were free. Their astral selves hovered over an old man. In front of him was a shattered crystal. There was fear in his eyes.

Jake sensed Mirim next to him and connected to the Matrix. Something was wrong back at the Citadel. They looked at the old man once more before they raced back.

CHAPTER SEVENTEEN - STAND OFF

Aras sat in the throne room, brooding. He could feel his power slowly slipping away. Adramelech was no longer under his control and his fleeting telepathic ability told him that something was going on with Ecu and Marta. He felt under siege on all sides.

If that wasn't enough, the boy was getting stronger by the day and he had escaped! The boy had to die. The pain was unbearable again. The thought of staying in bed for days because of it again was too much. The only way to cope was to leave his body for hours at a time. He couldn't live that way. The tablets Ecu gave him kept the pain at a tolerable level but at other times... He couldn't continue like this. His body was emaciated, he couldn't eat, couldn't sleep.

The lack of exercise was making him even more tired. He had to stop the Elementi before they destroyed him utterly.

A low bell sounded through the door to the throne room. Aras got up pressing his fingertips to his forehead. The room emptied, leaving only his generals.

Talik, his head of staff spoke, "All your ships are mobilized your majesty. *Fortune* is ready for you. The senior Magi Council have agreed to equip her with mages. We only need your orders now sir."

"You have the coordinates I gave you?"

"Yes sir, it will take us a day to get there."

"We must waste no time. You are dismissed." The generals began to leave the room.

Aras stood up. "Talik, a word before you go."

"Yes, my Lord?" The grizzled old general indicated for the others to go before him.

"I want you to do a favor for me first," Aras continued, "I want Ecu neutralized." A flicker of understanding passed between them and Talik left the room.

Calling for his coach Aras left the castle with confidence. Ecu would be taken care of. It was time to sort out the real threat. He wasn't going to miss this for the world.

Mirim and Jake fell into their bodies and scrambled up. They stiffly moved out of the chairs the others had dragged them into and looked at each other. Without saying a word they ran for the control room.

A being of fire stood by the control crystals. Its arms, consumed by subdued flame, were held around Kiera. A stranger stood arm's length away from him holding a red crystal. They seemed frozen in a tableaux. Where was Adra? Who was the boy? An arc of pure fire leapt from the fire being and enveloped the boy. Mirim tensed. He wasn't defending himself!

The fire withdrew for a second and Jake breathed in sharply through his teeth.

"Look at the crystal. That must be the real Fire King." Jake shouted. He ran forward, but the heat drove him backwards.

The boy fought back, determination evident in every line of his body but the Deoc just laughed and a fresh wave of heat filled the space between the stranger and Deoc. Kiera screamed and closed her eyes. Although shielded by the creature, she could still feel the searing energy wash over her. As she opened them again, she searched for the stranger. He was gone, his crystal falling to the floor. The Deoc swung around to face the new arrivals, dragging Kiera painfully with him.

"So *you* are the mighty Elementi? I don't think much of your Fire King. Who will be next?" The Deoc created a face of skin and bone and laughed at them.

Mirim strode forward.

"No you don't." Years of practicing her ability in the training rooms of the Citadel meant she knew exactly what to do. She concentrated on the Deoc's outline, pulling all the air from it while creating a barrier so no fresh air could flow back in. The Deoc's fire began to rescind. He changed back to his full natural form. The flames dimmed further as Mirim increased the pressure. Adramelech's holes for eyes widened in horror. He rose power from the core of his being, but there was no oxygen to fuel the flames. There was a slight hiss, and he disappeared.

Jake rushed forward and grabbed Kiera who was rubbing her neck.

"Are you OK?"

"Fine, but the boy - he was the Fire King - we don't have the fire element anymore." They all turned to look where Dani had fallen.

"Oh hell, we're stuffed now."

Just then the building stopped shaking and Shenella appeared by the blue crystals. Kiera looked out of the nearest side window. "I can see the top of the water."

They all rushed over. Shaking his head, Jake turned to Shenella.

"Shenella, can you organize the Merpeople to find out how close Aras is?" She nodded. He saw her turn her head. She was talking telepathically to someone he couldn't see. She turned back. "They are about twenty miles away from you."

Mirim's head jerked up "What!"

She hurried to the window. "Oh, gods. I can see them." In the distance, the horizon was filled with the shapes of tall ships. "There are hundreds of them!"

"Mirim, are they real? You said they have the power of illusion are they real?" Jake demanded.

"Yes, I mean no - I don't know. They could be real. There is no way to tell unless you are close up. They won't have any physical presence."

"Right. Shenella, ask some Merpeople if they will swim up close. Find out how many ships there actually are." Jake ordered.

She nodded. Her figure walked five paces to the left and disappeared into the wall.

"Okay, we need a battle plan and we need it quickly. Any suggestions?"

Kiera's thoughts whirled around. She disregarded her healing power. That would be useful later but not during the battle. What could she use to help them? She had control over volcanoes but that would damage them as much as their enemies. She had it.

"A force-field" she blurted out.

"Sorry?"

"I can use the planet's magnetic field to create a shield."

"Brilliant, at least we have some defense. Apart from the Merpeople is there anyone else who can help us?"

Mirim shook her head. "Everyone is too scared of the Empire. If we can defeat Aras, maybe we can change that, but for this, no."

Kiera took one of the high backed seats next to her crystals and sat back observing the others. "What powers do the Magi have?"

Mirim sighed. At least they were all there and she wouldn't have to say this again.

"They have the power of illusion and of course they can control Deocs. They don't want to control other elemental beings - just the fire. Maybe they don't know they can."

"So we have illusion and Deocs to worry about. The sun is starting to set now. If they arrive after it gets dark, they won't have as much energy to fight. We'll have to distract them somehow."

Shenella cut in. "They're ten miles away now."

"How are they moving so fast?"

He felt a niggling at the back of his mind. The Matrix - he'd forgotten about that. Allowing himself to connect fully again with the alien mind, he saw how he could get a better view. His panel was in the center of the semicircle. At the prompting of the Matrix merge, he concentrated on the middle of his desk. A wall of flickering white light rose opposite him against the wall. It expanded to produce a globe of light hovering above the ground. Pictures of the surrounding area outside the tower appeared within it.

Jake wished he could get a better view and the picture zoomed in on the ships. Mirim was right, there were hundreds of them. Fighting despair, he tried to get a better look at the ships. The picture responsively zoomed in again.

Everyone got up to take a closer look,

"Are you controlling this?" Kiera asked.

"Yes, through the Matrix - it's anticipating

what I want. Can anyone see Aras?"

The picture expanded again.

"There!" Shenella pointed. At the bow of one of the ships they could see a man point in their direction, as he talked to another man in a black uniform. It was either a general or an admiral, Jake guessed. Kiera looked from the image in the light and back to Jake.

"I know. Apparently we are related. He's my great-nephew or something." Jake explained.

Abruptly Shenella twisted around as if to answer an unseen call.

"Several of the temple guards have swum out to the ships. They swam through most of them. They report there are about forty of them that are real."

As she spoke Jake imagined the guards bumping into the ships. In response the picture behind them altered to show the bottom of the ships underwater. They could see three guards swimming together beneath the hulls. Through the churning water, they could see oars regularly beating the waves.

"That's how they are doing it - slaves." Mirim blurted.

Aras sat on his ship. The white towers of the Citadel rose from the sea, promising more power than he had ever dreamed of. He was half Elementi, and perhaps he could use that rather than fight it. Without a crystal he would not be as strong but if he attacked Jake, maybe he could beat him with the element of surprise.

As he had done hundreds of times before, he sat down and let his awareness float from his body. He sped towards the Citadel - following the white thread, which bound him and Jake together.

The four were talking quietly. It would be short-lived he vowed. He knew he had to act quickly, a part of him knew that if all five got together he would not have a chance. He couldn't see the fire element but he was sure he or she would be around. The dread at the pit of his stomach told him so. If he took down Jake, the others would crumble. He jumped into the boy's body.

Kiera was looking in Jake's direction when he faltered mid-sentence. As she watched he choked, his face turning red before he collapsed in front of her. From her console she reached out her arm. She could just touch him. She frowned; there was something... someone else there.

As she felt his arm, she experienced an overwhelming sense of pain and despair. She probed deeper. It was Aras! He was trying to take over Jake!

Kiera rushed over to Jake. His body convulsed on the floor. She grabbed hold of her crystal from the console and concentrated on it. As she held the small clear rock in her hand she saw two ghostly images superimposed on Jake's body. The two were evenly matched. Jake needed help.

Pulling the magnetic field from the ground deep beneath the ocean bed, she shaped it, altering it slightly and directed it at Jake's body. She watched the ghostly figure of the older man leave the limp body. Tuned to his frequency she followed Aras as he fled back to his ship. He was in so much pain, and she couldn't stand it. It was his Elementi side she saw. It was strangling him. Gathering her power again she once again tuned it to his resonance. She delved her awareness into his body searching for the tell-tale white stream of his Elementi power.

Kiera floated above Aras' body. This was the man who would kill them all if he could. But, he was in so much pain, would she be able to resist killing him? She could stop the entire war now. All she had to do was stop his heart. It would be so easy. It frightened her how simply it could be done. Just a little tweak here and all their problems would be over. She gave the idea room to roam for a moment. Deep down, the revulsion grew. She could never do that. Where did that thought even come from?

Reproaching herself, she began to focus her powers again. She gathered the magnetic field around her and sent small bursts of energy to unravel the white strand from around the darker stream coursing through his body. She hovered for minutes, ensuring it was completely free before blasting the cord with the power of Eleria's magnetic field. Satisfied the link was broken she left to re-join her own body. He wouldn't be able to do that again.

Moments later, Jake coughed and sat up. He shuddered at what had just happened. A thought occurred to Jake, he said aloud,

"Show me Aras."

The picture on the wall changed. This time, the uniformed man had gone. Aras was sitting cross-legged on the deck, a painted circle in front of him. He was murmuring something.

"What's he doing now?" Kiera asked.

"He's calling a Deoc," Mirim explained.

"No, he's calling several Deocs!" Jake shouted, and he pointed at the corner of the picture. The image zoomed in. Forty Deocs appeared floating in mid-air.

Shenella shivered in distaste. The fire-beings touched a deep-seated fear ingrained in her water-psyche. "There's one for each ship," she noted.

The Deocs hovered over the ships for a few moments, keeping pace with their speed. As one they moved off the ship and sped towards the Citadel.

Kiera ran back to her console. Placing her fingertips on her crystal she concentrated on the planet's metallic core. She could feel the energy radiate out in waves. She reached out and pulled it towards the surface. In her mind's eye she took the waiting schematic of the building from the Matrix and manipulated the energy to cover the surface of the Citadel. Increasing her pull, she felt the air fizzle around her.

"We have a force field," she called, "...but I have to concentrate on it to keep it up." As she spoke two of the Deocs reached them. They were heading straight for one of the windows. Expecting the crash of glass, they ducked; instead there was a large bang. As they hit the force-shield, the Deocs exploded.

Relief showed on everyone's faces. The

remaining Deocs halted in mid-air, seeming to consult one another and froze. Turning back to the ships, they could see Aras was summoning more of them.

"They may be able to get through if several try together." Mirim warned.

Jake hesitated. There was only one thing he could do.

"Are there any weapons here?"

"Weapons?" Mirim repeated.

"Yes, you know guns, swords, that sort of thing?"

"In the corridor, there should be some swords in the cupboards." Mirim stood and led him to the cupboard. She took out a small brass key from her pocket and unlocked the heavy wooden doors.

"Why is it locked?"

"Habit I suppose," she replied.

The cupboard was huge, spanning the entire corridor that split off at the far end into the Royal apartments. The section that she had opened held long heavy broadswords, standing upright in long rows. On the pommel of each sword was smooth white ivory. In drawers to the side were small daggers, each looking as expensive as their larger counterparts.

"Wow, I could have done with these when we were doing battle re-enactments!"

Jake saw her blank expression and shrugged. "Never mind." He grabbed the first one and tested its weight. It was half as tall as him but he swung the sword with practiced ease. It was well balanced. Happy with his choice, he ran back into the control room.

"Send me over to Aras."

"Are you sure? He will have been fighting with swords since he was a child," Mirim warned.

"So have I, Mirim, so have I."

Mirim looked doubtfully at him but nodded. She placed her hands on the crystals and Kiera copied her. Jake nodded at them and a swirling mist of light began to surround him. It brightened and he gave a brief brave smile before he disappeared from their sight.

Karl chose that moment to join them at the control room.

"Was that Jake?"

Kiera nodded. "He's gone over to fight Aras."

"Are you mad?" Karl looked from the image on the far wall. "There is more than one man on that ship. He'll be killed before he even gets to him!"

"We can't fight that way," Mirim replied.

"I can. Send me over to help." Karl ran out of the room and grabbed a sword from the open cabinet visible from where he stood.

Running back to the control room, he shouted at Mirim.

"Send me now!"

"You've got no powers, you'll only hinder him," Mirim protested.

Karl rolled his eyes.

"He's fighting with a sword, not any powers. I can help."

"...In for a Hars, in for a Heral." She nodded at Kiera and they touched their crystals again. Karl was gone.

The air was still on the ship when Karl materialized, but the ship was still rocking slightly. It took a second to get his bearings before he looked up to find his friend. He grabbed hold of the railing for support when a large sailor spotted him. With a roar the man lunged at him with a dagger. Karl ducked and brought his sword up in a swift sharp jab to the kidneys. The man collapsed yelling. Karl paused, breathing hard. He'd never hurt anyone before. He'd 'killed' while fighting but that was play-acting. This was real.

A shout to his left brought him out of his reverie. Jake was in trouble. Karl left the man groaning and leapt over a barrel that had rolled towards him. The seas were getting choppy. Mirim and Shenella were using their powers to distract. Problem was it was distracting him as well. He smiled grimly; he knew what was happening though. Any advantage was a good advantage.

Jake had managed to get to Aras, but Karl could see another sailor out of Jake's line of sight about to strike.

"Jake! Behind you."

Jake turned with surprise to see Karl, nodded in recognition and looked behind him. Jake threw up his dagger, reversing it, before shoving it behind him. It sliced through the air and pierced the man's stomach like butter. Still in his hand, he threw it up again to reverse it to parry a thrust from Aras. Jake was good!

More sailors came up the ladder from the decks below. Karl groaned. He charged forward and met the first one. They fought, parry after parry. The other man was bigger and drove Karl back, step by step, but Karl was quicker. Eventually Karl found himself back to back with Jake.

"This is like old times," grunted Karl.

"A bit more dangerous," Jake muttered in return.

Jake had never been more happy to see his friend. They moved as if choreographed. Each knew how the other would react after years of fighting mock battles together. His friend spun off fighting two sailors, one with the sword he brought and the other with the dagger he'd picked off from a fallen foe.

Jake turned back to Aras. He was a good fighter. But the older man had been ill and the strain was starting to show.

"Why are you doing this?" shouted Jake. He brought his sword above his head to avoid another fatal blow.

"One of us must die." Aras aimed low. Jake jumped to the side but tripped over a rope. He fell heavily. Aras shouted, seeing his chance. Jake rolled on to his side and swept his legs against the other man's, tripping him up. Aras fell trying to grab hold of a rope. He missed. A sailor fighting Karl bumped into him from behind and Aras fell forward over the railing. They heard him yell as he fell into the sea. A roar erupted from the higher deck. Jake looked back for his friend.

"We have to go Karl; there's too many of them. Aras has gone."

Karl ran over to him and looked overboard - there was no sign of the Emperor. Turning quickly he brandished his weapons at the advancing guard.

"Take us back!" Turning to the men advancing Karl shouted.

"There can be only one!"

Jake groaned at his friend. It wasn't as if any of these had ever seen any films, let alone Highlander! Shaking his head, he took out his crystal and connected to the Matrix.

"Kiera, Mirim, bring us back!"

Lights swirled around them, became brighter and Mirim was sat in front of them.

"You made it!"

Jake moved off and took his place beside the other two. Karl moved off to the corner of the room to watch. The scenes on the screen in front changed as they watched to see what was happening now that Aras was gone. To their horror more Deocs were appearing above the ships. There were hundreds! By unseen command, the Deocs moved together as one towards the Citadel. Jake looked at Mirim.

"They don't need Aras!"

There was a large crack above them and the sound of shattering glass. Kiera's grasp of the shield collapsed.

The room was suddenly filled with Deocs. Jake acted quickly. He grasped them all into a mind merge and created a dome of power over their heads. The Deocs flew over them, obviously incensed.

"I can't hold them for long!"

Karl was standing under the shield. He wished he could help. Beside his foot, Karl felt a surge of heat. He looked down. It was a crystal, just like the others were carrying. Curious, he bent to pick it up. It was warm to the touch and red fire swirled in its depths. Images began to form in the flames. The pictures shattered and reformed in his mind as the crystal gently glowed. Memories began to surface. He gasped as he remembered. He was the Fire King? The boy - he saw what had happened now. The boy was a cousin. He was family. Karl's eyes burned as he realized the only family he had left died before he ever knew him.

Jake's shield glowed white and it lowered against the combined power of all the Deocs. The Matrix urged Karl through the crystal. He jumped at the unfamiliar intrusion and remembered that he had been connected before when he was a child. Karl hadn't had time to be trained before he was sent to Earth, but his father had shown him a couple of tricks. He knew what to do.

Feeling for the familiar energy of fire, he concentrated on the nearest one. As he focused inwards, he matched his energy signature to the Deoc in front of him. Its yellow eyes briefly blazed with sudden fear as it realized what the boy was doing. To the others he seemed to melt towards the boy and flow into him.

Jake looked blankly at his friend.

"How?"

"I'm the Fire King, you idiot. I was sent to Earth too but I never had the crystal. It was given to my cousin when a Deoc took him to safety thinking he was me. I remember now. Kind of explains why I didn't think it was too weird that you could read minds, doesn't it?"

Karl twisted and a few more Deocs flowed into him. He was invigorated. All that raw energy. It was amazing.

"It's working!" Mirim exclaimed.

Emboldened, Karl concentrated on the other creatures. It truly was exhilarating, the energy sucked in from all sides. To the others he glowed a deep red with the energy. As each Deoc disappeared, they heard a small fizzle.

Kiera recovered from the shorting of the

shield, began gathering the magnetic field again. This time she grimly thought it was going to be strong enough to beat off five hundred of those things. The air shimmered around her. Jake let the dome drop. An opaque green shimmering light surrounded the Citadel.

"It won't stop anything physical, only energy," she warned.

"Impressive." Jake put his hand out of the broken window. The light fizzled but let him push it out and back in again.

Suddenly they heard a crash. As they were linked to the Matrix, they instantly knew one of the outer buildings had been hit. Rushing back to the light screen they saw what must have been a general directing cannon fire at them.

"They're about a mile and a half away; we need to do something quick." Jake ducked instinctively as another cannon ball shook the Citadel.

"Mirim, Shenella, can you create a storm? We need to sink those ships before they get any closer."

They nodded. He watched them sit back at their consoles deep in concentration. As he watched, clouds from miles around began to move towards the ship. The water began to get choppy. Still in the mind merge, Jake could feel the tremendous energies played by the two.

"Kiera, you need to keep the shield up. They'll probably send more Deocs now they know they broke through the first shield." As he spoke more were forming beside the ships. "Karl, you need to create lightning. If we can punch a hole in the hulls, maybe we can sink them quickly."

The storm was building in front of them but they still needed to charge the clouds. Jake dipped into Kiera's shield and sent a bolt of energy up to the clouds a mile away. Karl caught it with his mind and separated the charge turning the upper clouds positive and the lower negative.

The waves below were now thirty feet high, and the ships were going out of control. The sailors who were manning the cannons, rushed to the sails to help stabilize the ships. Without the cannon fire, the Elementi were able to redouble their efforts. The charge built up in the clouds and Karl aimed at the first ship. A crack and jagged lightning hit the mast and the first ship began sinking. The sailors took hold of rigging and swung to safety to a nearby ship. The mage at the aft was unable to jump in time. A lightning bolt hit him and fifty ships disappeared. Everyone cheered.

Talik was standing on the deck watching with horror. He never realized their power was that strong. He rang the ship's bell. His men scrambled to grab hold of the ropes, sails moved as they used the wind to their advantage. They regained control of their ships.

The Merpeople reported to Shenella that only five ships remained. It was time to get serious.

"Grow the storm," Jake ordered. Mirim inclined her head and increased the wind, Shenella moved the water in its path, and together they created a giant whirlpool. The ships juddered in the water. The mages suddenly lost interest in fighting the Citadel and fought to stay on the decks. Huge waves crashed against the sides of the ships, sending men overboard. On the view screen in the Citadel they saw four ships remaining.

Jake sent up another bolt to the clouds, energizing the electrical field. As the energy built up Karl shaped them into bolts and sent them down on to the ships like acid rain.

"I feel like Zeus!" Karl shouted.

Bolts of lightning crashed from all directions above them to the waiting ships below. Shenella aided by Mirim created a tsunami and watched it grow and roll into the whirlpool. The ships veered from side to side and moved faster as the waves crashed in. Karl and Jake joined forces and sent in one more bolt of lightning, blinding them for the moment before destroying the whirlpool and the ships trapped inside it.

All five stood there stunned.

The whole battle had only taken half an hour.

They stared at one another grateful to be alive. Outside the sky was clearing as they let go of the pent up power. There was no trace of Aras or his ships. Slowly, they looked back at one another.

It was over.

EPILOGUE

The next day, the sky was bright and clear. As Mirim waited by the door, she released a sigh of happiness. She had done everything her mother had asked of her; the Elementi were together and they would rebuild what was once lost.

A splashing to her left announced the arrival of Shenella with a companion. Irritation briefly flew across Mirim's features but she hid it before the girl could see it.

"Good morning, Your Highness." Mirim smiled brightly.

"It is." Shenella replied looking around. As she spoke, water dripped off her. Her clothes were as dry as if she'd hadn't come out of the ocean just seconds ago. "This is Sori, my advisor and friend."

Sori looked startled at bring described as a

friend. As well he should thought Mirim. One did not make friends with advisors. He shouldn't even be here!

Mirim nodded and led Shenella and Sori up the main staircase into the meeting room where the others were gathered. Three of the five chairs were already occupied. Evenly spaced around a circular table the chairs were engraved with family symbols on the headrests.

Shenella gratefully sunk into the seat with the fountain crest while Sori stood with his arms folded behind her.

Jake immediately gave Mirim a glare and stood up to dive out of the room. Everyone jumped at the sudden movement. Karl smiled when he realized what Jake intended. Moments later Jake returned, dragging back a chair from the anteroom.

"We're not having any of that elitist stuff here." He placed the chair by Shenella's nodding at Sori to sit.'

"Jake!"

"Yes?" His eyebrow soared up to his hairline.

Mirim backed down. "Your Majesty."

"Karl and I talked last night, and we think that we are going to have a go at this. Kiera was right when she said we wouldn't return to much on Earth. Here, here we can help people make this world a fairer place."

Shenella smiled and looked at Sori. "This new king is nothing like Aras," she 'pathed to him.

"You are right. We are in for some interesting times, Your Highness," Sori replied silently.

Mirim looked quizzically at the pair. "I can't hear you." She was confused. "I can tell you are talking but I can't understand what you say."

Sori smiled. "It is a natural function of the Merpeople. Your Highness, we are able to converse telepathically in secret and it is the skill of the water power to understand us, something which perplexed your ancestors. We all have skills the others need, and that is why the Elementi were so strong when you were united."

"Whatever, people, we are here to talk about what to do next. Aras is gone..."

"Did you see him die?" interrupted Mirim.

Kiera rolled her eyes. "Let Jake speak, Mirim."

"As I was saying, Aras is gone but the Capital is still under the control of the Magi. The wizard who captured Mirim and me is still around and we need to bring the peoples together."

"The wizard could also tell Aras' cousins in the Dark Continent," interjected Sori.

"...so we need to think about what we are going to do next. I, Karl and Kiera don't really know this world, whereas Shenella and Mirim were brought up here."

"We need to recover the chain."

"Sorry, Mirim?"

"The chain, it was always with the Focic crystal. It is a technology long gone but it magnifies your power so you can magnify one of the elements to the strength one of us holds." Mirim spread her arms out to the rest of the table. "It must have got lost or at least given to someone for safe keeping. It was powerful in its own right and they wouldn't have risked sending that to Earth. It may even have been possible for a human to control an element with the power of that. Not the way we can, but enough to cause trouble."

"Not to mention the Dark Continent. Someone will have to go there and see if they know what has happened and if they do what they plan." Kiera said quietly referring to Sori's earlier point. "That probably should be Shenella as she has had experience in a court. Our world hasn't had that set up for centuries."

Everyone turned to Shenella and her heart sank. Not again. She bowed, "That is true I have been in Aras' court for a few years and I know what is expected."

"We also need to know who the people will support us in a fight if it comes to that." Karl chimed in.

"Yes we will need to go to each of our ancestral people and regain their trust. They have suffered greatly in the last one hundred years." Mirim replied.

"We have a plan, everyone. Let's go do it!"

ABOUT THE AUTHOR

Ceri Clark was born and brought up in Aberystwyth, Wales in the UK. After a brief flirt with the UK Ministry of Defense, a cruise ship and a waxworks museum, she spent years working as a Librarian in private and public libraries which has given her a love of stories and books she hopes to pass on to her son.